Bad
to the Bone

By Melody Mayer

The Nannies

Friends with Benefits

Have to Have It

Tainted Love

All Night Long

Bad to the Bone

Bad to the Bone

by Melody Mayer

Delacorte Press

a nannies novel

All rights reserved. Published in the United States by Delacorte Press, an imprint of
Random House Children's Books, a division of Random House, Inc., New York.

Delacorte Press is a registered trademark and the colophon is a trademark of
Random House, Inc.

Visit us on the Web! www.randomhouse.com/teens
Educators and librarians, for a variety of teaching tools,
visit us at www.randomhouse.com/teachers

Library of Congress Cataloging-in-Publication Data
Mayer, Melody.
Bad to the bone: a nannies novel / Melody Mayer.
p. cm.
Summary: Seventeen-year-olds Esme, Lydia, and Kiley, nannies to the stars,
juggle their complicated personal lives with the demands of taking care of the
children of the rich and famous in Beverly Hills, California.
ISBN 978-0-385-73518-6 (trade)—ISBN 978-0-375-89132-8 (e-book)
[1. Nannies—Fiction. 2. Interpersonal relations—Fiction. 3. Friendship—
Fiction. 4. Beverly Hills (Calif.)—Fiction.]   I. Title.
PZ7.M4619Bad 2009   [Fic]—dc22   2009001655

Printed in the United States of America
10 9 8 7 6 5 4 3 2 1

First Edition

Random House Children's Books supports the First Amendment
and celebrates the right to read.

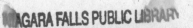

With gratitude, for Wendy Loggia,
always steady at the helm.
The kind of person my great-grandfather
would have hired in a Hollywood second.

Bad
to the Bone

Kiley McCann

Kiley McCann looked up at the giant *H* in the Hollywood sign, which loomed above her head. Instead of feeling thrilled, she just felt nervous.

"We shouldn't be doing this," she muttered as a Los Angeles Police Department helicopter buzzed by in the distance, the *whop-whop* of its spinning blades cutting cleanly through the air as it sped west toward Beverly Hills. The "this" to which she referred was being inside the fenced area around the famous white letters, high in the Hollywood Hills, because being inside the fenced area was most definitely illegal.

Her friend Lydia Chandler smiled beatifically. "We're doing it as we speak, sweet pea," she drawled in her faint Texas accent. "Just relax. I know it's hard. High anxiety runs in your family."

Esme Castaneda's dark hair brushed her shoulders as she looked around, cautious as always in an unfamiliar place. "Kiley's just being rational. If you don't want to get arrested, rationality is good. And I definitely don't want to get arrested," she added.

"Y'all, life is too short to stress," Lydia insisted as she spread her arms wide. "The City of Angels is at your feet. Just look at it!"

For a brief moment, Kiley took her friend's advice and gazed out from their perch above Los Angeles. It was a rare smog-free late-summer day in Tinseltown, thanks to a gusty onshore breeze; the view stretched from Alhambra in the east all the way to the Pacific Ocean in the west, with downtown L.A., Koreatown, West Hollywood, Beverly Hills, Brentwood, and Santa Monica in between. Off in the distance were the oil refineries and bustling harbor of Long Beach. How clear was it? Kiley could make out the long line of passenger jets coming in over the city in preparation for their landing at LAX.

I was on one of those planes, she thought, *not that long ago.* She'd arrived with a tattered backpack, her neurotic mother, and a whole lot of dreams. And now, she lived here—as nanny to the children of a famous rock star. She had friends—Esme and Lydia, who were also nannies. And perhaps most unlikely of all for a pretty average girl from small-town Wisconsin—at least, that was how she saw it—she had a famous boyfriend, a model/actor about to shoot his second film.

Kiley would have taken a moment to relish all that, along with the spectacular view, except that said view was so very illegal. Well, not the view so much as the shady perch from which they were taking it in. Lydia had coaxed them through a small hole in a protective fence topped with barbed wire, and dozens of large signs reminded them that what they were doing was against the law: NO TRESPASSING! TRESPASSING IS A CRIME AND YOU WILL BE SUBJECT TO ARREST BY THE LAPD!

Kiley gulped, realizing that she and her friends were not the first people in Los Angeles to be tempted by this very place. The police probably had cameras set up in the hillside brush just to catch people like them, and were probably on their way right now. Great. She'd always wanted to see what a Los Angeles lockup was like from the inside.

Not.

"Just ten minutes," Lydia was assuring her as Kiley looked cautiously at Esme. Esme had grown up in Echo Park, a tough, gang-riddled Latino neighborhood in East Los Angeles. She had more experience with the LAPD than anyone ought to have. Her ex-boyfriend, Junior, had been a gang member.

If it was okay with Esme, she'd stay. Otherwise, Kiley would obey her clutching stomach and be outta here. She cut her eyes at Esme. "Well?"

"Y'all aren't chicken, are you?" Lydia asked innocently.

"Oh please, *chica,* do not try to psych me out," Esme snapped. She sighed, then added, "Ten minutes, it's fine. We're not a high police priority. But we shouldn't stay more than that."

Lydia punched the air with happiness, and Kiley wondered if Lydia had, in fact, psyched Esme out. If there was one thing Esme wanted to be in this world, it was tough. Strong. Fierce. All this Kiley knew.

"So," Lydia began, "let's review. A week ago, we said we'd

3

meet up here and talk, because we all had big things to decide. Now, here we are. Which means it's time to spill. Who wants to spill first?"

Kiley leaned back against one of the walls of the giant *H* and folded her arms, hoping that her body language said that she didn't want to talk first. Where would she even start? She was nothing more than a semi-cute girl from La Crosse, Wisconsin, one size bigger on the bottom than on the top, with auburn hair and a sprinkle of freckles across her nose. She'd come to L.A. to take part in a television reality show that would select the next nanny for the aging rock star Platinum and her three kids by different fathers (no one knew who those fathers were, and what with her being famous and rich, speculation about the baby daddies only increased Platinum's cachet). The TV show had tanked before it ever made it on air, but Kiley had been hired by Platinum anyway and installed in a gorgeous guesthouse behind Platinum's huge Bel Air mansion.

Over the course of the summer, she'd taken care of Platinum's kids, begun a romance with a gorgeous male model named Tom Chappelle—his near-naked torso adorned numerous city billboards in an advertisement for a famous brand of underwear—and been the star witness at Platinum's trial for reckless endangerment of her own children. That case had been tossed just before it went to the jury when the drugs and drug-taking paraphernalia that were key evidence disappeared from the evidence room at police headquarters. The judge had had no choice but to free the rock star, albeit with the pronouncement that in his humble opinion, she was incredibly guilty on every count.

Now Kiley was at the start of senior year at Bel Air High School, with the goal of applying that fall to be part of the freshman class at the Scripps Institution of Oceanography down near San Diego. Scripps was the real reason she'd even tried to become Platinum's nanny. With in-state tuition, going there was a possibility. As the out-of-state daughter of a Wisconsin brewery worker and his diner-waitress wife? Ha. She couldn't even afford books and supplies.

She had no doubt about the best part of her summer—aside from meeting Tom. It was having become best friends with Lydia and Esme. She knew they were an unlikely trio, though all three of them were nannies for rich and at least semi-famous Hollywood families.

Lydia worked for her aunt Kat Chandler, a former professional tennis player who until a week before had been the longtime lesbian lover of her then domestic partner and former tennis rival, Anya Kuriakova. They'd had two children via artificial insemination, Martina and Jimmy. Last week, Kat had discovered that Anya had been cheating on her . . . with a guy. That was the end of their relationship. It was a remarkable story, but even more remarkable was that Lydia herself had spent the last eight years in the Amazon rain forest, where her parents—former rich Texans—were medical missionaries in a small village of primitive Amarakaire tribesmen. Lydia was bilingual, in English and Ama. Of medium height, with choppy blond hair, petite features, and an enviable figure, Lydia dripped cool despite—or perhaps because of—her unconventional upbringing. She'd met a great guy over the summer, an aspiring scenic designer named Billy Martin. Lydia wanted nothing more than to continue to lead the Bel Air lifestyle to which she was rapidly becoming accustomed. For now, she was a senior at Bel Air High School with Kiley.

As for Esme, the backstory was no less unlikely. A little taller than Kiley, with thick, glossy dark hair, penetrating dark eyes, and lush curves, Esme was the daughter of a Mexican couple who had crossed into America without papers and were now the caretaker and housekeeper for famous Hollywood producer Steven Goldhagen and his second wife, Diane. Esme was a talented tattoo artist who'd recently opened her own studio in Century City. During the summer, she'd been hired to be the nanny for Steven and Diane's two newly adopted Colombian twins, Easton and Weston. That was fine, except she'd fallen in love with the Goldhagens' actor son, Jonathan. When Esme and Jonathan had a falling-out, Esme had resigned herself to focusing on her tattoo business. Her parents had wanted her to stay in school—she was supposed to start at Bel Air High School with Kiley and Lydia, and her mama and papa wanted nothing more than for her to be the first person in their family to go to college. But Kiley knew that Esme was now getting six, seven, eight hundred dollars, sometimes even more than that, for a freehand tattoo that she could do in two hours. When they were poolside at the country club, actresses and models approached her without being prompted, basically begging for a tattoo, willing to pay any price to be at the top of her list.

That had to be tempting, Kiley thought. As Hollywood nannies, they were all making five hundred a week, plus room, board, and a nice car to drive. (Except for Lydia, who didn't have a license. BMWs and Mercedeses weren't big in her part of the Amazon, and the only real road was the piranha-infested Rio Negro.) To make fifteen hundred bucks in a night for doing body art? Kiley couldn't imagine.

"Come on, come on," Lydia urged, pulling Kiley out of her musing. "Time's a-wasting. Who's going to be first? Kiley, you have to tell us what you've decided to do with Tom. He's supposed to go away to Russia to do this movie. Esme, are you going back to work for the Goldhagens?"

"What about you?" Esme shot back. She was wearing flip-flops, cut-off jeans, and a blue tank top. Her beautiful tawny skin glistened in the warm afternoon. "You met that guy Flipper last weekend, but I think you're still in love with Billy. What are *you* going to do?"

"I'll go second," Lydia pronounced. "Kiley?"

Kiley gulped. She hated being put on the spot. "I'll go third."

"You guys are wusses," Esme said. "It's not that big a deal. Okay. I wasn't sure until right now. But you've inspired me. I know I won't see you hardly at all if I live in the Echo and just go to my business. If I go back to the Goldhagens' to work, we can hang a lot more. So I think I'll go back."

"All right!" Lydia shouted, and threw her arms around Esme. "You're going back to the Goldhagens' and you'll go to Bel Air High with us and—"

Esme held up a palm to stop Lydia midsentence. "Wrong. I'm not going to that tight-ass rich kids' school, ever."

Kiley frowned. Esme was so smart. And her parents had sacrificed so much so that Esme could go to college and succeed—how could she possibly let them down by dropping out?

Esme squirmed away from Lydia, who had issues with

personal space in the sense that she didn't recognize that such a thing existed. Lydia's sensibilities had been honed in the rain forest among primitive tribesmen who were a lot more touchy-feely than . . . well, pretty much everyone. In fact, Lydia had related that the Amas cupped other males' scrotums when meeting them for the first time. It made Kiley glad to be a girl.

"But school," Kiley began tentatively. "If you don't finish—"

"Why should I finish?" Esme interrupted. "I make more money now doing tattoos than I ever could, even if I went to business school, which I never would. What's the use of high school?" She said these last two words as if they were somehow polluted.

"Your parents won't be happy." Kiley knew how much the Castanedas longed to have Esme finish her education.

"My parents don't have to live my life. I do. What about you, Lydia?" Esme turned to her blond friend. "How's high school so far? Broken any hearts lately? Has Billy called you? Or maybe I should ask if you've called him?"

Lydia laughed. "I just love how you cut right to the chase, Esme."

"There's no time to screw around. We've got about three more minutes before we get out of here."

"Oh poo," Lydia scoffed. "High school is fine. Easy. Kat took the kids up to San Francisco for a while, so I've got the place to myself. And no. I haven't called Billy."

"Has he called you?" Kiley asked. She knew Billy and liked him. Not only did he look like Tom Welling from *Smallville*, but he was also a true gentleman.

Lydia hitched up her red and white shorts, which bared

the tops of her hip bones and were much shorter than Esme's. With the shorts she wore a U2 T-shirt. Kiley figured the shorts were by some famous designer, as Lydia knew and cared about such things. Of course, her friend couldn't begin to afford clothes by famous designers, so she "borrowed" things from her aunt's closet.

"No phone calls in either direction," Lydia continued. "And you know what? It's fine."

"Really?" Kiley asked.

"Sweet pea, there are just too many hot guys in this town to be so limited. I mean, I've only had sex with two of them and one doesn't count."

Kiley knew Lydia didn't want to talk about her very ill-advised one-night stand.

"I'll go out a few times with Flipper. Or maybe some other boys. I'm seventeen! I don't think I'm made to settle down." She turned to Kiley with piercing green eyes. "Your turn. And don't dodge. What are you gonna do about Tom when he's in Russia?"

Kiley knew she had to respond. Her friends had been so honest about themselves, and she wasn't sure what was even going on with Tom. After a small part in the summer block-buster *The Ten,* he'd been offered a major role in *Kremlin Cowgirl,* a Russian-American coproduction about a young Russian entrepreneur who opened the first country music honky-tonk in Russia. In the movie, Tom was to play a young cultural attaché at the American embassy who befriended Boris, the entrepreneur. Dolly Parton was also involved in the project, and Tom's love interest was Chloë Sevigny, who played an American expatriate.

The problem was, Tom's departure for Russia kept getting postponed. Originally, he was supposed to leave the previous Monday. Then it was Wednesday. Now, his plane was to leave in two days. In some ways, this was worse than him just leaving in the first place.

"What I want to know is, are you and Tom going to see other people?" Lydia asked bluntly.

Esme nodded. "How long is the shoot?"

"Seventy days." *Seventy days,* thought Kiley. That felt like an eternity.

"Enough time to get into plenty of trouble," Lydia observed. "I'd need about seventy minutes."

"Not helpful," Esme chided. The sun was a little lower in the sky now; she backed away from the rays, up the hill a little bit.

"I agree. Because I don't know what to do."

Kiley felt anxiety well up in her throat. Tom was a great guy. If you took away his amazing looks—his chiseled chin, blue eyes, tousled sandy hair, and a body like a professional athlete—he was just a boy from Iowa whose parents grew wheat and corn and who was used to waking up before sunrise to care for the cows and horses. But taking away his amazing looks was like taking the smile away from the Mona Lisa. That was to say, impossible.

"Well, don't fret, Kiley. You'll figure it out," Lydia assured her. "And if you don't you can always pass Tom over to me. I swear, he's the hottest guy I've—"

"Attention, attention!"

A metallic voice, obviously amplified by a bullhorn, boomed out over them.

"Shit," Esme said. "Why did I ever listen to you, Lydia?"

The sinking feeling in Kiley's stomach reached oceanic depths. There could be no doubt who was responsible for the bullhorn voice. But if there was, the next sentences confirmed it.

"Attention, attention! This is the Los Angeles Police Department. You are trespassing on city property. Come out immediately, with your hands up!"

"What do we do?" Kiley hissed, frantic.

Esme's eyes met hers. "We do what the man says. We do it slowly, and we do it now."

Kiley watched as Esme held her hands high over her head and started back up the narrow dirt path to the hole in the fence. Then, she did the same, with Lydia following.

There had been a lot of firsts for her here in Los Angeles, and now she was about to rack up another one. Her first arrest.

2

Esme Castaneda

Esme eyed the two young cops. The scowls on their faces said they meant business. One was tall and blond with high cheekbones and thin lips; the other was a few inches shorter, with dark hair and the square jaw of a superhero, or, this being L.A., an actor who played a superhero. If one had been Latino, maybe Esme could have done the "Yo, homey" thing in Spanish, and tried to talk them out of arresting her and her friends. But they were both gringos, so she didn't stand a chance.

Why had she let Lydia talk her into something as stupid as going inside the fenced-off area? Her life was a series of near misses with law enforcement. She'd taken a stupid chance. And for what? To prove that she wasn't chickenshit? Just when she'd finally made the decision to go back to the Goldhagens'.

Just when her tattoo business was taking off. Everything would be ruined over this stupid, stupid decision. Plus, her parents were going to kill her.

"Did you girls not see the signs?" the shorter of the cops barked. "No Trespassing means no trespassing!"

"We're really sorry," Kiley whispered. It was clear to Esme she could barely get the words out of her mouth.

"Save it," the taller cop snarled. "Sorry is no excuse. You girls are in big trouble."

Double shit on a shingle. Well, Esme was not about to crawl. Whatever happened, happened.

"Is it a felony?" Kiley squeaked.

"What, you think this is some bullshit little misdemeanor thing like jaywalking, missy?" the gruff cop spit.

Lydia blew her shaggy blond bangs off her forehead with a puff of air. "Dang, it's hot out. So wait, a misdemeanor is the not-so-scary one and a felony is like real, real bad? Because I always get them mixed up. Like felony and fun start with the same letter? So I always think that's the one that isn't some big-ass deal."

The shorter cop glared at her. "Are you effing with me? Because you do *not* want to eff with me."

"She's not from around here." Esme defended Lydia automatically, although she didn't know why she was being so charitable. This was all Lydia's fault.

Meanwhile, Esme saw that Kiley was shaking like a fault line during a temblor. "Please don't arrest us. We'd lose our jobs and get kicked out of school and—"

The superhero cop was unmoved. "Should have thought about that before you flouted the laws of this great city. Now

13

I'm reading you your rights. You have the right to remain silent. Anything you say can and will be used against you in a court of—"

"Oh officers," Lydia trilled. "There must be something we can do to kind of fix things?"

Then, very slowly, she reached down to the bottom of her U2 T-shirt and began to lift it, inch by inch.

You cannot be serious, Esme thought. Lydia was about to offer sexual favors to two of L.A.'s much-less-than-finest, in return for dropping the charges. Not only was it unbelievably stupid—the LAPD had come a long way since the ignominies of the Ramparts division scandal years ago, when this kind of maneuver would have worked—but it made her want to puke. She'd rather be arrested a hundred times over than go that route. "Don't," she muttered. "Just don't."

If she'd thought her words would have any effect, she thought wrong. Lydia continued undeterred. Another inch of tan, slender abdomen came into view. Back in Amazonia, Lydia—of the full and perky perfect breasts—barely ever wore clothes, much less a bra. Soon that perky perfect pair would be bare to the world. And they'd still get arrested. Esme knew from experience: you did not mess with the LAPD.

"Lydia, stop," Kiley pleaded.

"You want this on your permanent record?" Lydia replied as her shirt rose another inch. "What's Scripps going to think? What are you going to put on your college app when you get to the question 'Have you ever been—' "

That was all Esme heard. Because the end of Lydia's sentence was suddenly drowned out by very loud recorded music, booming from a wooded area twenty or thirty feet away

14

from the clearing. She recognized the song—it was on the radio all the time. Who was in the woods blasting music while she and her friends were about to be arrested?

It was just bizarre. But not nearly as bizarre as what happened next.

"Oh man, I love this song," the blond cop announced, and began to bop his head to the beat.

"Yeah. It's hot," the shorter cop agreed.

"So hot," said the superhero cop.

"Totally, totally hot." The short one nodded. Then, he began swaying his hips to the music, his nightstick knocking into his meaty thigh. To his left, the tall cop unclipped his handcuffs from his belt and started waving them overhead, thrusting his pelvis as he did.

Suddenly, Lydia—as if she was some kind of entranced, arrested zombie—started dancing toward the cops, her body writhing sensually, her hips swaying at least as suggestively as the two policemen.

"Lydia! Get back here!" Kiley was aghast.

"Lydia! *Basta!*" Esme shifted unconsciously to her native Spanish.

It was to no avail. As if this was some sort of bizarre and twisted dream, Lydia started dancing with the two cops. Then, to Esme's shock, the taller cop danced right back over to her, tossing away his nightstick, handcuffs, and cap, and unbuttoning his standard-issue cop shirt. He had a chiseled and hairless chest underneath. The shorter cop opened his own shirt in three quick movements and joined his partner in the dancing.

That was when Esme put her hands down. No way was

she staying in the "You're under arrest" position with two ass-hole rogue cops stripping. She glanced down at her cheap pink espadrilles and cursed her decision not to wear sensible shoes to meet her friends. Running from these insane cops in espadrilles was going to be damn tough. Kiley, she noticed, had on her usual Converse All Stars.

"What's going on?" Kiley implored.

"Damned if I know," Esme replied. "Don't move till I do. But put down your damn arms. They don't care."

Now the cops were unzipping their pants, and Lydia was clapping and catcalling as if she was in a strip club. "Take it off, baby!" she yelled. "Take it all off!"

Esme had had enough. "Let's go!"

She tugged Kiley's arm; together, they started to sprint for the trees. But at that same moment, a third cop moved out from the grove of trees, laughing and pointing a video camera at the dancing cops and Lydia. The music cut off; the cops and Lydia stopped dancing and froze in their exact positions.

Esme and Kiley stopped running—because the two cops and Lydia were now doubled over in laughter, and so was the young policeman with the video camera. He had spiky black hair, intense blue eyes, and the cut, trim body of a competitive swimmer.

"Ohmigod," Kiley breathed. "I know that guy."

"Who?"

"The so-called cop." Kiley pointed to the third policeman. And then, inexplicably, she started to laugh too.

"What's going on?" Esme demanded.

Kiley could barely get the words out. "I think we've just been—"

"Punk'd!" Lydia pointed a finger at Kiley and then at Esme. Meanwhile, the policeman with the video camera kept filming.

"That's her friend from school, Flipper," Kiley filled in, nudging her chin toward the guy with the camera. "This has to be a joke."

A joke? Lydia had set them up and it had all been a joke?

"Y'all should see your faces right now," Lydia chortled.

The blond cop was still doubled over laughing. "I'm Evan," he said, when he could finally speak. "We go to school with Flipper. That was freaking hilarious."

He made his way over to Esme and extended a hand. "No hard feelings?"

"Asshole!" Esme stomped on his foot as hard as her espadrilles would allow. There were some things you joked about and some things you didn't. When you grew up in Echo Park, and the police were seen as the enemy, you did not joke about being arrested.

"Damn, that hurt!" Evan yelped.

The other "cop" held his palms up. "My name is Daniel—don't stomp on me, babe," he joked.

By now, Flipper and Lydia had joined them, and Flipper had put down his video camera.

"You planned this?" Kiley asked Lydia.

Lydia nodded. "I told Flipper we were meetin' up here and we kind of planned it together. Don't be mad. Come on, it was funny!"

Esme thought for a moment. Even if she and Kiley had

been the butt of the joke, it was a hell of a lot better than really finding themselves under arrest. "Okay, it was kind of funny," she admitted.

"Yay, I knew y'all couldn't be mad," Lydia insisted. "And I have the greatest idea."

"I think maybe I can live without any more of your great ideas," Kiley responded.

Lydia shook her head. "This is my best idea yet. Look on YouTube tomorrow. We're all gonna be famous!"

When Esme had worked for the Goldhagens, she'd had her choice of fabulous cars—they had a BMW, a Lotus, a Jensen Interceptor, a Mercedes, a classic DeLorean, a Maserati, and a few others Esme had never driven. Now, as the automatic gate opened at the bottom of the private drive that led uphill to Steven and Diane Goldhagen's massive Bel Air estate, she drove her friend Jorge's ten-year-old Saturn SL2. Her parents, who were doubtless already here and on the job, had an even older car, a 1997 Toyota Corolla that was as trustworthy as it was rode hard. Last time Esme had checked the odometer, it had registered 250,000 miles.

Before her falling-out with their older son, Jonathan, Esme had loved being nanny to the Goldhagens' newly adopted twin daughters. Mostly, she related to their cultural confusion. Until June, Easton and Weston had had Spanish names and lived in an orphanage in Cali, Colombia. While an orphanage in Cali was quite a long way from rugged Echo Park, they were both very foreign to the privilege of Bel Air. At least the twins had learned English quickly. In three months in America, they'd become largely functional. Diane Goldhagen had hired Esme because she was both trustworthy and bilingual.

Diane herself was one of those aggressively thin, aggressively blond Hollywood second wives who were considerably younger than their husbands and who divided their time between self maintenance—this was nearly a full-time job in and of itself—and various high-profile charities. She'd met the twins on a trip to Colombia, and decided to adopt them immediately. This was an easy process, not the least of which was because of her famous husband. Steven Goldhagen was right up there with David Kelley, Dick Wolf, and the late Aaron Spelling for his clout and success in Hollywood.

Diane had brought the twins home to new names, a new country, a new family, and a new older brother—Jonathan—who had also been Esme's boyfriend. Trying to get over her breakup with him was just one of the things that had led to Esme quitting her nanny job. The Latina hired help falling for the rich gringo son was just too disgusting a cliché. Still, she missed him.

Leaving Jonathan was why she'd left the twins. It was wrong. She was ashamed she'd considered only herself when she quit. But she was making so much money with her freehand tattoos—one Hollywood person told another one, who told another one, who told another—that she didn't need the nanny money. Her going rate right now was eight or nine hundred dollars a tattoo.

Still, leaving the Goldhagens was about a lot more than the money. Her pride had caused her to quit. Her pride caused her to do a lot of things, but not always the right thing.

The gate swung open and admitted her to the estate that had been her home. The winding road was just as she remembered it; the flat circular parking area by the white mansion held the Mercedes, the Lotus, and the Maserati. Her parents' Toyota was there. She knew it would be parked by the workmen's shed, below the tennis court and beyond the guesthouse where she'd lived when she was an employee.

Nothing had changed at the house that she could see. The bougainvilleas were in better bloom, and the huge mahogany door had been freshly waxed. The air was redolent of fresh flowers. Not three miles away, the city of Los Angeles teemed with traffic, smog, and noise. But here, in the hills to the north, the Goldhagens had created an oasis of privilege.

She was just about to ring the doorbell when the front door swung open. Steven Goldhagen himself stood there to greet her.

"Esme!"

He hugged her as if she was a long-lost daughter. Around age fifty, he was on the short side of average, slender, with two days' growth of brown and gray beard and gray eyes to match. He wore a tattered NYU sweatshirt with the sleeves cut off, baggy no-name jeans, and an old New York Mets baseball cap to cover his balding head. This was how a top Hollywood producer did business. Esme knew that the town did not stand on ceremony, and that the only ones who dressed like businessmen, in crisp white shirts and ties, were the agents.

"Come in, come in," he urged her, leading the way into the family room, which had recently been redone in American Indian décor, complete with headdresses on the walls and an authentic sand painting on one area of the floor. "Diane is out with the girls, Jonathan's together with his agent, so it's just me. I was so glad you called. Have a seat."

"Thank you." She perched on the edge of the new couch; this one was deep, ruby red leather dotted with black and white pillows. "And thank you for agreeing to see me," she added.

Steven joined her on the couch, his lanky arms dangling. "I'm having a busy day. Problems on the new CW show. How about if we cut to the chase? I know today is deadline day. Want your job back?"

Esme had practiced what she wanted to say in the hopes that it would make her less nervous. She took a deep breath, and launched into her pitch. She felt she had made a mistake in quitting and regretted her decision. She realized it made her seem flighty to come back just two weeks later asking for her old job, and she was sure Diane had hired someone by now, but perhaps they needed a second nanny, which was the arrangement they'd had once before, and—

Steven cut her off. "You're right. Diane went through an agency and interviewed a dozen girls. We hired a grad student at USC. Nice girl, nice family—or so we thought. Turned out she was a nightmare with the booze and the drugs and the twins hated her."

This was bad news for the Goldhagens, but Esme hoped it was good news for her.

"You fired her?" Esme asked.

"Two days and she was out of here. Then we used temps from another service—all British—the twins couldn't understand them. And Monday, Diane has a dozen new girls to interview from some other agency." He made a dismissive gesture. "Don't ask. I get TV shows made easier than this nanny search. So if you want your job back . . . welcome home."

Esme could hardly believe it. "Really?"

"Really-really. I'm up to here with the RMAs—I'm producing this year. I have no time for domestic trouble." He rubbed his temples wearily.

"RMAs?" Esme asked.

"Rock Music Awards, on Music Television Network. In fact, I'm thinking maybe you can help out. Your friends too, if they have the time."

"I could ask them."

"Great," Steven said. "The girls are starting school at Crossroads—can you believe they're going right into first grade, no ESL?—so you'll have quite a bit more time. I know about your tattoo biz—the whole town knows about your tattoo biz, I think—but I could use some people around I can trust. Nothing glamorous, mostly gofering and ushering and being a minder. But half the people in this town I wouldn't trust to flush the toilet after they piss. You know what I mean?"

Whew. Esme thought that was quite a speech, maybe the longest she'd ever heard from Steven, ever. On the other hand, working on an awards show could be interesting.

"I . . . yes, of course I know what you mean. So . . . just like that?"

"Just like that. Pick up your keys and move back into the guest cottage. Just one thing."

She knew what he was going to say. *Stay away from Jonathan.* The hired help does not date the son of the lord of the manor.

"Yes, sir," Esme said.

He waved his hand again. "Enough with that sir business. It's Steven. The one thing is: don't ever quit on us again. Deal?"

"Deal."

Huh. It wasn't about Jonathan. Though Esme thought he had nothing to worry about on that score.

Steven rose, so she did, too. He held out his hand and she shook it.

"The twins are going to be happy. Welcome home, Esme."

He got a set of keys and handed them to her, then walked her to the door. "Move in when you want. The guesthouse got cleaned after Miss Druggie moved out, so it's waiting for you."

She thanked him again, and walked on the gravel path she'd trod so many times, past the clay tennis court where she'd first seen Jonathan playing with his old girlfriend, around the bend to the quaint guesthouse. Two bedrooms, dating back to the golden age of Hollywood, with exposed wood beams, a parquet floor, and a bathroom with antique fixtures that she'd come to love. She stood in front, inhaling the scent of orange blossoms, taking it all in: the riot of flowers, the black benches, the basketball hoop in the driveway out front. She recalled all the times Jonathan had snuck into her little house so that they could be together, even though his stepmother had expressly forbidden it, and so Jonathan had finally moved out and gotten his own place. She thought about the dreams she'd had in that cottage, the simple dinners she'd cooked when she wasn't eating with the girls at the main house, the all-night talks with Lydia and Kiley, all of them sprawled on the living room floor.

She had missed it here. So much.

The front door of the cottage opened. A uniformed maid, her hair in a tight bun, pushed through the screen door. She had a mop in one hand and a bucket in the other. She looked tired. Very tired.

"*Hola, Mama*. I'm back."

And then she went into her mother's arms.

3

Lydia Chandler

Lydia sat forward on the chaise lounge next to the Olympic-sized pool in her aunt's deserted backyard and remembered what Billy had told her about how to open a bottle of champagne.

"If you don't want a geyser, don't twist the cork," he'd advised. "Hold the cork, twist the bottle. Slowly. It works every time."

Well, she might not be with Billy anymore, but this was a great time to try out his advice. Kat and Anya—well, Kat, now that Anya was gone—had a wonderful wine cellar full of hundreds of bottles. Red wine, white wine, wine from France, wine from Chile, wine from California. It was odd, because neither of them were big drinkers at all. Lydia had checked out the cellar thoroughly, and discovered several cases of

Taittinger champagne. A little Internet research revealed that Taittinger had a stellar reputation. She decided there was no time like the present to check out that rep.

"It's just you and me," she said to the bottle. She tore off the foil top, unscrewed the wire cork-protector, took hold of the top, wrapped a small towel around the bottle—it was a warm night, and condensation had formed on the chilled glass—and gave a twist.

Pop! The cork released with a minimum of spillage. Dang if Billy wasn't right. "Let's give 'er a taste."

She lifted the bottle to her lips, tilted it back, and tasted. Billy had also told her that the French monk who discovered champagne had exclaimed, after his first swallow, that the drink tasted like stars.

That monk was right. The Taittinger was heavenly. Lydia sighed and took another long pull. Mmm. Fabulous.

She was all by herself in her aunt's expansive backyard. In addition to the swimming pool, there was a tennis court modeled after the ones at the National Tennis Center in New York; a hot tub; a paddle tennis court; a shaded area with enough exercise equipment to outfit a gym; a gazebo; a pool house with sauna, steam room, and changing quarters; and house telephones at every turn in case anyone wanted to summon more drinks, more food, more anything. There was 24/7 staff up at the house that wanted nothing more, and was paid for nothing more, than to make anyone on the premises happy.

Not only that, she had the place to herself for two whole weeks. Her aunt Kat, right after working as a television color commentator at the US Open tennis tournament, had come back to Los Angeles and immediately packed up the

Mercedes. She, her daughter, Martina, and her son, Jimmy—named for former tennis stars Martina Navratilova and Jimmy Connors—were taking a drive up to San Francisco for a couple of weeks. Yes, the kids would miss the first weeks of school. But they were both good students, and they could stay in touch with their teachers by e-mail.

Lydia felt for them. Kat and Anya had been a longtime couple. They started out as rivals on the tennis court and became lovers, and then, partners. But then Anya cheated on Lydia's aunt. With a guy. When Kat found out, she went ballistic. Anya moved out, which left Kat partner-less and the kids second-mother-less.

On the other hand, Anya was a ballbuster, constantly making to-do lists and leaving the kids with no freedom. Lydia didn't like her. Also on the other hand, the split-up gave Lydia the estate to herself for half a month. Her aunt's driver, a great guy named X, was at her beck and call. The cook, Paisley, would whip up whatever Lydia wanted. The housekeeping staff did her laundry and cleaned up after her. All she had to do was wake up and let X take her to school, which was what she'd done since school had started last week. Mostly. Growing up in Amazonia hadn't made attending school a big priority for her. There seemed to be no good reason to make it a priority now.

So mostly, she was living the life to which she thought she should become accustomed. She sipped her champagne and smiled. This was a helluva long way from the mud huts of the Amazon. She picked up a copy of the *Universe,* a popular tabloid, and idly leafed through it. Lindsay Lohan, the Olsen twins, reality show stars, a piece on the upcoming Rock Music

27

Awards because the *Universe* was sponsoring a contest where the winner would get two front-row seats and backstage passes. After weeks of breathless reporting about Platinum's reckless endangerment trial, which had put her friend Kiley into the spotlight too, it was as if the scandal had never happened.

Lydia sipped more champagne and threw the tabloid aside. Funny, really. Everything in her new life was disposable. In Amazonia, no one disposed of anything. Everything was recycled, including magazines, which became toilet paper.

Lydia sat up, pulling off her clothes—the champagne was making her feel really warm—and jumped into the crystalline pool. Floating on her back, she gazed up at the dusky night sky. Dang, what a great life. She had everything she could possibly want. Except . . . someone to share it with.

She swam to the lip of the pool, where she'd left the champagne bottle, and took a long pull. Back in the Amazon, she was rarely alone. There were always Amas around, or her own parents, or visiting doctors on do-gooder missions. You couldn't get away from people after dark, because wandering into the rain forest alone could turn you into some wild beast's premidnight snack. Lydia wasn't used to being alone. And she didn't much like it.

Well, then. She'd just have to do something about that.

Platinum's floodlit estate was white. Very white. Blindingly white, Lydia thought as she walked up the white gravel path that led to the front door while X pulled away in the Beemer. It was only a ten-minute drive from her aunt's estate over to Platinum's, but living in the rain forest had made it tough to get a driver's license. She had to call X to take her there, and as usual, he did his duty with a smile—and plenty of dish on who was hot and who was not this week in Hollywood.

Lydia had pulled on bleached-out tattered jeans that fit her like a second skin, and a lavender silk Stella McCartney camisole "borrowed" from her aunt's latest swag bag. She didn't even have to ring the bell. Kiley was waiting for her, dressed in khaki shorts and a white University of Wisconsin–La Crosse T-shirt.

"Thanks for letting me come over. I got lonely," Lydia confessed. "And I just wasn't in the mood to go party with strangers at some club."

"You? Not in the mood to party?" Kiley teased.

"I'd probably meet some guy and dance and get rowdy and think about sex and then maybe even *have* sex, which, as you know, I am trying not to do until I get to know someone real well," Lydia explained earnestly. She'd been accused of being honest to a fault. But she didn't see how being honest could be a bad thing.

"Didn't want to call Flipper, huh?" Kiley asked.

Lydia shrugged. "He's off at a swim meet in La Jolla."

Kiley hugged her. "Well, I'm glad you're here. Come on in. There's something amazing happening."

Lydia perked up, sensing new tabloid fodder. She'd spent so many years in a mud hut reading about the wild exploits of the rich and famous, she couldn't help being excited now about actually living among them.

"Platinum spreading lines out for her kids?" Lydia ventured. "Or are they breaking up a key of cocaine together?"

Kiley made a face. "Thankfully nothing like that. Platinum's got a visitor. Come and see. Or should I say, come and hear."

As Kiley led the way through the white-on-white foyer, down the white-on-white main hallway, and into the white-on-white living room, Lydia paused a few times to check out some of the Platinum memorabilia that adorned the walls. She'd been to Platinum's place several times, but always went straight to Kiley's guesthouse in the back, never inside the main house. There were blown-up magazine covers, Grammys, and awards certifying that her records had gone gold or platinum. They were in English, French, even Russian. Platinum's career had spanned three decades. While she didn't have the same popularity as she did twenty years ago, she had definitely crossed into the realm of rock icon.

"Want something to drink?" Kiley asked, motioning to the white marble bar at the far end of the living room.

"I don't know," Lydia admitted. "I've had plenty of Taittinger—"

"You drink Taittinger?" came a female voice with a British accent. "I adore Taittinger. Could live on the bloody stuff!"

Lydia turned. The speaker was petite, with short, shaggy ebony hair and shaggy bangs that nearly obliterated the kohl-lined dark eyes in her pale, heart-shaped face. She wore black capris, a pair of black rubberized clogs, and a Tottenham Hotspurs soccer jersey. Above that, her slender neck was covered in tats; Lydia couldn't make out what they were from across the room. She did, however, know who the girl was. Not for nothing did Lydia steep herself in all things pop culture.

"You're Audrey Birnbaum!" Lydia exclaimed.

"So I've heard," the girl agreed. "You a fan?"

Was she ever! Audrey Birnbaum was the newest, hottest R & B singing sensation from Liverpool, not far from where the

Beatles had grown up. Audrey's aunt had even been Paul McCartney's girlfriend, many years ago. Audrey was twenty-one, and she'd been discovered singing in a pub by the same people who had turned Rihanna into a major star. Audrey was famous for her husky voice and her wild ways, or at least that was what the media claimed.

"Am I a fan?" Lydia echoed. Then she began to sing the lyrics to Audrey's latest hit, "Can't Remember Your Name":

"You sent me a breakup letter, I stoked it and never smoked better, you're up in flames, can't remember your name, boy, can't remember your name. . . ."

Audrey laughed. "Not much of a voice but yeah, that's my song."

"Audrey Birnbaum, meet my friend Lydia Chandler," Kiley said. "Audrey's working on a duet with Platinum for the Rock Music Awards."

"And it's bloody hard work," Audrey added. She plucked a pack of smokes from the rear pocket of her capris and tapped out a cigarette, then offered the pack to Lydia. "Smoke?"

"That stuff'll kill you," Lydia pointed out.

"Yeah? Hadn't heard," Audrey said breezily, lighting up. She exhaled smoke toward the ceiling. "So Lydia, what do you do besides look hot?"

Lydia beamed. "You think I look hot?"

"I imagine the whole world thinks you look hot, chicklet," Audrey opined.

"You know, I take that as a great compliment, you being bi-sexual and all," Lydia said.

Audrey laughed and flopped onto the white tapestry couch. "You read that in some rag?"

"That's kind of personal," Kiley put in quickly.

"As if I care," Audrey commented. "I was bi before bi was hip, sweets." She flicked ashes into her cupped palm. "Which team do you play for?"

"Sorry?" Lydia had no idea what Audrey meant.

"You like girls or boys or both?" Audrey asked.

Lydia noticed that Kiley was blushing, which Lydia found sweet. These kinds of questions didn't bother her in the least. The irony was, she was usually the one asking them, not the one being asked. She shrugged. "I love my girlfriends to death, but not like that. I love boys, though. I got started kind of late on account of I used to live in the Amazon, where the guys were five feet tall and had no teeth. So now I'm makin' up for lost time."

Audrey burst out laughing. "Get out. Are you shitting me?"

Lydia assured the singer that she was definitely not shitting her, and rambled on about her unique upbringing. Audrey seemed to find it fascinating, and kept asking Lydia questions, which Lydia was more than happy to answer.

"Where the hell did you get to?" Platinum said, striding into the room, dead-eyeing Audrey. "I come back from the john and you're gone."

The superstar wore white jeans, a white tank top, and understated makeup to go with her trademark long, stick-straight, glossy blond hair. Lydia thought she looked well, especially for someone who had spent much of the summer in pretrial detention. Platinum noticed Lydia and gave her a little wave, which Lydia returned. And that was it, as far as getting noticed was concerned.

"I was hanging with your nanny and her friend, sweets,"

Audrey explained, putting out her cigarette on the bottom of her flip-flops. "This girl's fabulous."

"Flirt later, work now," Platinum demanded. "We need to fix the harmony on the bridge."

"Great." Audrey rose. "Kiley and Lydia can be our first audience." She crooked a beckoning finger. "Come along, sweets."

Lydia's cell dinged with a text as Platinum and Audrey led the way to Platinum's home recording studio. She'd check it out later; she was too excited right now. The singers put on earphones and ran the sound through the system so that the instrumental blared from state-of-the-art speakers, and then the two women sang along.

The song that Audrey and Platinum had written was a driving rock-and-roll power number with an infectious, hooky chorus. Lydia could tell it had been inspired by Platinum's experience in the criminal justice system. Come to think of it, Audrey had a little experience in that arena, too.

> When you're safe in the arms of justice
> Never think you're safe at all.
> Freedom is love, love is freedom
> Loving freedom is the best of all . . .

Lydia found herself bopping her head to the beat, and even humming along to the chorus. As for Platinum and Audrey's voices, they soared and twisted together like two hawks riding the summer thermals above the desert. It sounded as though they'd been singing together their whole lives.

When the song ended, Kiley and Lydia applauded loudly. "That was fantastic, y'all!" Lydia exclaimed.

33

"I loved it, too," Kiley agreed.

Platinum nodded. "It was okay. I'm still not happy with the bridge."

"And the second verse. I want to move around some of the lyrics," Audrey told her.

"Yeah. And I'm not happy with that 'Loving freedom is the best of all' shit," Platinum declared.

"I like it. It's kind of Janis Joplin–Bobby McGee–ish," Audrey mused.

"Needs work, I'm serious," Platinum insisted. "Kiley, call Mrs. Cleveland, tell her we want cappuccino and a fruit plate."

"A fruit plate? You mean, like with kiwis and blueberries?"

"As opposed to the ones with steak and ravioli," Platinum quipped.

Audrey stuck out her tongue. "Bitch."

"Love you too." Platinum turned to Kiley. "Add a bloody rare burger with chips for the British bitch over there."

"And a six-pack. I can't write without beer," Audrey said. "We'll save other illegal substances until we're done."

Both superstars laughed. So did Lydia. This was just so cool! Kiley excused herself to give the order to Mrs. Cleveland. Platinum moved over to the white grand piano and noodled some notes. Audrey hung with Lydia, lighting up another cigarette.

"So luscious Lydia," Audrey began, "I was thinking. Platinum and I are working tonight, but I'm definitely partying tomorrow night. Maybe you and Kiley want to come with? Do some clubbing? I might meet up with some of my industry friends. You know Beck?"

Whoa. Was this really happening? Had Audrey just asked

her and Kiley to go clubbing with her and Beck? "I'm there," Lydia declared. "I'm sure Kiley will want to come too. Her boyfriend is leaving tomorrow to do a movie in Russia. We can help take her mind off of it."

"Audrey? Work?" Platinum demanded from the piano.

"Don't get your knickers in a wad," Audrey groused. She winked at Lydia. "Tomorrow, then. Get my digits at the hotel and call me." Audrey moved off to work with Platinum just as Kiley returned from placing the food order.

Lydia beckoned Kiley into the hallway so that they wouldn't disturb the singers. "Audrey just invited us to party with her tomorrow night!" she exclaimed.

"That's nice," Kiley said.

"Nice?" Lydia echoed incredulously. "It's amazing!"

"You go," Kiley urged. "I won't be in the mood."

"Mooning around over Tom," Lydia guessed. "Well, if you change your mind . . ."

"I won't," Kiley said.

Lydia sighed. "Okay. Then let's talk about something really important. Like tomorrow night. What am I gonna wear?"

Kiley laughed at that. Which was exactly what Lydia had intended.

4

"So Audrey Birnbaum is just as out there as everyone says she is, huh?" Tom asked as he brought Kiley a Diet Coke from his minibar. She was sitting on the taupe velvet couch in the living room of his new suite at the Hotel Bel Air. The carpet was plush aquamarine, the floors and counters of the kitchen slate gray marble, the two bedrooms done in ocean colors. When Kiley had been a contestant on *Platinum Nanny*, she and her mother had been ensconced in the suite next door to Tom's. In fact, that was how they had met. But since Tom's career had heated up, he'd moved to one of the corner suites.

"Well, she chain smokes, that's for sure," Kiley mused, sipping her drink. She'd filled Tom in on the night before with Platinum, Audrey, and Lydia. "And she made some joke about illegal substances, so maybe all the stuff you read about her is true. I mean, imagine having that kind of talent and then trashing your life."

"Kind of like Platinum. No wonder they're friends." He sat next to her and took a long pull on the bottle of beer he'd opened.

Kiley smiled. "But so talented. You should have seen them working together on their song. You know, I remember when Platinum wanted to be *your* fast friend."

Once, when Tom had showed up at Platinum's estate to take Kiley out on a date, Platinum had flashed him. She'd been drunk at the time, which just proved Tom's point. That was before the trial. Since then, Kiley hadn't seen Platinum touch a drop of alcohol, a joint, or a line. It was a new Platinum.

Tom leaned close and brushed his lips against the side of Kiley's neck. "Not interested. Wasn't into her then, not into her now." He smoothed back a few auburn hairs that had escaped from her ponytail, and kissed her ear. "Got my eye on someone else. . . ."

Me, Kiley thought.

Even after all these months, every time she saw Tom and took in the incredible hunkiness of him—the blond hair, intense blue eyes, and cleft chin; the square shoulders and long, lean muscles; the entire package that had girls and women all over the world sighing and swooning over his now infamous underwear ads—she found it hard to believe that he had chosen her. That she was his girlfriend. That she'd finally had sex for the first time and he was the one with whom she'd had it.

And that it wasn't just sex. It was so much more. Love. It felt like love.

But. Tom had never said those words. And neither had she.

"You hungry? We could order room service. Or delivery. There's a great new Indian restaurant on Sunset. Killer Curry. They deliver." He ran one of his fingertips over her lips.

Indian food? Kiley thought. *That's what's on Tom's mind the night before he leaves for Russia?*

Finally, the tickets had been sent over by the producer. Tom was booked on an eight a.m. flight to Moscow; principal photography would start on his film the day after tomorrow. Yet he was as casual with her as if he was shooting the movie in Los Angeles, as if they wouldn't be apart at all. Or maybe— this was the part that made Kiley's heart feel like a beached carp flopping around inside her chest—this was casual like a guy who wasn't in love at all.

"Maybe later," she replied, determined to keep things as light as he seemed to want them kept.

"Works for me." He leaned in and kissed her softly. She closed her eyes and gave herself up to it. Soon the tender kisses grew more passionate. He tugged her T-shirt over her head, and reached around to unclasp her decidedly uncool white racer-back bra.

She mentally chided herself. Why hadn't she bought some fabulous lingerie? Why didn't she think about things like this ahead of time? What about her panties? Bikini with polka dots. She'd tried a thong once and had deemed it a torture de-vice. Now Tom was reaching to undo her jeans, and she real-ized that her polka dot bikini panties were not exactly going to fill him with lust. Lust was what she wanted him to feel when he thought of her and he was on the other side of the world surrounded by gorgeous, ready, willing, and—Kiley had no doubt—extremely Russian girls who would long to make Tom feel right at home in Red Square.

"Hey." Tom's eyes peered into hers.

"What?"

"You okay?"

"Sure."

"You seem like you're a million miles away."

"You're the one who's going a million miles away," she said, trying to keep her tone light.

He kissed her again. "That's tomorrow. I don't want to talk about tomorrow. Come on."

He stood and reached out a hand for Kiley. She took it and he led her into the larger of the two bedrooms, kissing her as he gently laid her on top of the seafoam quilt, which covered a king-sized silver four-poster bed. The only light came from the twinkling stars and a three-quarter moon shining through the picture window. Tom's hands were everywhere. His lips took Kiley's breath away. There was nothing in the world but that moment, that guy, until she thought all the stars in the night sky were exploding, and after that, she didn't think at all.

Kiley awoke in Tom's arms. His body curved around her, his lips buried in her neck. The bedding was a mess, the pillows on the floor. How had that happened? She smiled. Right. Now she remembered how it had happened. How long had she been asleep? She craned her neck, trying to catch a glimpse of the clock radio on the nightstand without waking Tom.

"Hey," he whispered hoarsely. "What time is it?"

"Can't see the clock." She turned in his arms so that she was facing him. "Did I wake you?"

He kissed her forehead. "Sleeping is overrated."

"But you have to get up so early." With an international flight at eight, he'd have to be at LAX by six. That meant leaving the hotel at five.

"My ticket's first-class, courtesy of Worldwide Pictures. I can sleep on the plane." He reached over and adjusted the Bose clock radio so that he could see the face. "It's just ten. Time's on our side."

"Ten," Kiley repeated dully. That meant they had only seven more hours. "Do you still need to pack?"

"Did it already. Not taking much. You know me, I'm still a farm boy at heart. Mmmm. I'm going to miss this."

He tugged her toward him and started stroking her bare back. She nuzzled into his warm, hard chest, wondering what he meant by "this." Did he mean he'd miss sex? Or did he mean he'd miss her? If he meant her, why hadn't he said "I'm going to miss *you*"? But he couldn't mean he'd miss sex—that would be laughable. He could hook up with half the former Soviet Union if he wanted to. Why shouldn't he? It wasn't as if they'd ever talked about being monogamous. Not that Kiley would ever, ever, *ever* have sex with another guy while she was involved with Tom. She didn't want anyone else. But that didn't mean Tom—

"Uh, Kiley?"

"What?"

"Something is going on with you."

"No, nothing."

40

"Yes, something. Is it Platinum? Is it the kids?" He rolled over onto his back and regarded her thoughtfully in the moonlight.

"No, no, they're good. Surprisingly good, actually."

"What is it, then?" He gently massaged her right shoulder. "You're so tense."

She knew what she wanted to say, but she didn't dare. "Please don't have sex with anyone else while you're in Russia. All those amazing Russian girls, with their cheekbones and clingy dresses and would you please take me to America, you rich and famous American model, I'll do anything for you? When they smile at you, please don't smile back."

There was more. She wanted to ask him if he loved her. But that was even more out of the question. Too awkward. Too blunt. Too needy. She had zero experience with this kind of thing. Why hadn't she thought to ask Esme or Lydia how to handle it? Not that Lydia would be able to help. She'd basically torpedoed things with Billy. Esme—Esme would know what to do.

"I'm fine. I was wondering how you think it'll be, working with Chloë Sevigny?" Kiley asked, going for casual. Chloë struck her as a sexy free spirit, someone daring. Someone who might just get involved with her handsome costar.

"Great. The table read was awesome. We're on the same flight. It'll give us a chance to get to know each other better."

Swell.

"And now that Jessica Simpson is doing a cameo—"

"Say *what*?"

Tom's brows knit together. "Didn't I tell you about that?"

"No."

"Yeah. I thought everyone knew. She's this big star who shows up out of the blue on opening night to help Boris get the honky-tonk off the ground. Supposedly she met him when he used to be a Moscow cabdriver. That's the backstory. She plays herself."

"I guess it won't be a stretch, then," Kiley managed.

"Guess not. I haven't met her yet but my agent says she's a sweetheart."

Kiley tried to recall the last things she'd read about Jessica Simpson. Was she still with the Cowboys quarterback? Lydia would know—she always knew all the celebrity gossip. Even if Jessica was involved with someone, what if she also wanted to be involved with Tom?

First a country full of beautiful women. Then Chloë. Now Jessica. Kiley felt like barfing. She glanced downward at her very visible, slightly rounded stomach. Jessica's stomach was washboard flat. So was Chloë's. She reached for the sheet and tugged it upward to cover herself.

"Don't," Tom said, reaching for her hand, which held a bunched-up hunk of sheet. "You look so beautiful in the moonlight."

"I'm cold," Kiley lied, and settled the sheet over both of them. "We'll text each other, right?"

"Yeah, sure. I'll be really busy, though, and I'm not sure what kind of cell reception I'll get over there. So if a few days go by and you don't hear from me, it won't mean that I'm not thinking about you."

Maybe he really would be thinking about her, but Kiley knew she'd be thinking about him more. She'd read some-where that in every relationship, one person always loved more, and the other person was loved more. If that was true, then it was clear to her who loved more in her relationship with Tom. She *hated* that, feeling all insecure and needy. She felt certain that it had to be wildly unattractive. She felt just as certain that a guy like Tom wanted a girl who didn't need reassuring. Why couldn't she be more like Esme, who was never insecure when it came to guys? If she could just be more like Esme, this whole situation would be so much easier. She asked herself: *What would Esme do?*

The answer was obvious. And it made a whole lot of sense, especially if she could deliver it in the most offhand, casual tone she could muster.

Kiley was standing her ground.

"So I was thinking. While we're apart? It's perfectly fine to see other people."

He cocked his head sideways a bit. "That's what you want?"

She wanted to scream the truth: *no!* But he wasn't saying he didn't want to see anyone else. And if he wasn't saying it, how could she?

"I just don't think there should be this pressure."

He looked confused. "Pressure to what?"

"I know how it is on a movie set. Well, I mean, I've read about it. It becomes its own world for a while. That's the world you'll be in. And that's okay with me."

"It is?"

"Sure." She forced herself to smile and kiss him lightly. "It'll end, you'll be back, and we'll see what we see."

"If that's what you really want . . ."

He pulled her close again and kissed her temple, then closed his eyes. That was when she realized that he was dozing off again. How could he? She'd just given him a green light to hook up with whomever, and he was perfectly fine with that idea.

Soon she heard him snoring softly. It was a long, long time before Kiley could sleep too. When Tom's wake-up call came, he went in to shower while she stayed in bed, sadder than she'd ever felt. When he finished and pulled on jeans, a T-shirt, and an ancient brown leather bomber jacket that had once belonged to his dad, Kiley was dressed and waiting for him. She'd made coffee in the suite's coffeemaker, and handed him a cup.

He took a long sip, then put the coffee down. "You don't have to leave. Why don't you go back to bed?"

"I do have to leave. I've got school, and the kids, and it's too sad to be here without you."

Whoa. That was honest.

"Hey." He used a forefinger to tilt her face up to him. "I won't be gone that long."

"Sure, I know. And I'll be so busy I won't even realize you're gone."

So much for honesty. Talk about telling a big, fat lie.

They left the suite together. The hotel grounds were empty at this hour, almost as if it was a movie set. Kiley thought that if it had been a movie, it would be some chick-flick weepy where the heroine—her—won't admit how much she loves the hero.

A black car was waiting for Tom at the hotel entrance. Tom handed his bag to the waiting driver, a thin middle-aged man with steel gray hair, who put it in the trunk. Then Tom snaked his arms around her and kissed her. "I'll miss you."

"I'll miss you too." She kissed him again, then broke away quickly, fumbling for her car-check tab in her purse so he wouldn't see the tears that were welling up in her eyes. She forced herself to smile brilliantly and wave as the car pulled away, carrying Tom and her heart with it.

5

"May I have your attention, please?"

Steven Goldhagen banged a spoon against a martini glass and then held the spoon overhead, motioning for everyone to settle down. There were over a hundred people in the banquet room at the Beverly Hills Hotel for the production luncheon for the Rock Music Awards, and there didn't seem to be much of a response to Steven's request for the noise level to drop to where he could easily be heard.

Esme leaned toward Lydia. "They ought to let him talk. He's paying for everyone's lunch."

"Maybe they're talking about how good it was," Lydia replied. "Course, four months ago I was eating monkey meat, so almost anything that comes out of an actual kitchen tastes good to me."

It was Friday afternoon; Esme and Lydia were at the RMA kickoff luncheon at the Pink Palace, which was what everyone in Hollywood called the venerable Beverly Hills Hotel. With the award show coming on Saturday night, Steven had decided to do a morale-building luncheon for the entire production staff. At breakfast that morning, while Esme was getting Easton and Weston ready for school, Steven had expounded on his theory of show business as a team sport. That is, it was as important to build morale in your employees as it was to keep morale high on a basketball or soccer team. Hence this luncheon, for which Steven and the other producers had pulled out all the stops.

The room itself was decorated beautifully. One of the nicest banquet spaces in the hotel, it had a huge crystal chandelier and a ceiling that was easily three stories high. There were four long tables where crew members sat; each table was covered in a custom-made RMA tablecloth. Along the walls were posters from the five previous RMA shows, plus television monitors that replayed memorable moments from them. Esme had seen quite a few of these, and especially remembered the Carlos Santana and Coldplay jam a few years back. At each person's seat was a commemorative Rock Music Awards program, plus a small bag of swag. Esme had checked hers out. There was a unisex tank wristwatch, a pen-and-pencil set, and a small video recorder that could record up to thirty minutes. Everything was engraved with the latest RMA logo.

As for the food, it was just as impressive as the décor. They'd started with cold oysters on the half shell, followed by a delicious tomato-spinach soup that somehow had been poured so that there were separate swirls of orange tomato and creamy green spinach liquid. Then came the main course, fresh rockfish caught that same morning by Santa Barbara Island and helicoptered to the hotel (this Esme knew because she'd been in touch with the caterer to help coordinate the event), plus an icy cucumber-and-dill salad from the hotel garden, and *pommes frites*—which was a swanky way of saying they served french fries. There were white and red wines from Napa and Sonoma counties. Dessert had been a dozen different kinds of mini donuts from Sweet Hole on Sunset, currently *the* place for dessert in Los Angeles. Esme had eaten half a dozen of the delicious confections. The best had been the hazelnut cream.

Now, as Steven still tried to get his crew to quiet down, white-jacketed waiters were pouring coffee from French press makers, as well as a variety of herbal teas. Lydia had opted for coffee, while Esme was content to finish her glass of iced tea. She smiled when Lydia plucked yet another mini donut from the platter in the center of the table. Lydia was one of those girls who could eat anything and everything—and she did—and never gain an ounce.

"Blackberry," Lydia reported as she bit into the tiny donut. "Lord, I have died and gone to heaven." She washed it down with some coffee. "Too bad Kiley is missing this."

Esme had invited Kiley, too, but Kiley had opted to go to school instead. On the other side of Esme sat a chattering group of hairstylists, makeup artists, and dressers. It seemed that half of them were named Heather and the other half Kelly.

It turned out that there had been some advantages to being Steven's personal production assistants, which was how Steven had told Esme and Lydia to refer to themselves.

"If anyone asks, you're special assistants to the producer," he'd instructed.

One of the Heathers and one of the Kellys had asked

immediately. The answer that Steven had provided was sort of a golden ticket. For the rest of the meal, Esme and Lydia were treated like demigods.

Up at the head table, Steven had started a discussion with a bald man in an expensive Italian suit, so everyone had started talking again.

Lydia looked at her watch. "I'm late to my English class." She shrugged. "Oh well."

"You shouldn't just blow off school," Esme said.

Lydia's eyes widened. "Look who's talking."

"I already have almost all the credits I need to graduate."

"'Almost' only counts in blow darts, sweet pea," Lydia said sweetly. "An 'almost' high school diploma doesn't count."

Esme turned away. She didn't want to think about the fact that she'd dropped out of school. It was bad enough that she'd disappointed her parents; she really didn't want to be teased about it by her friends, too. Besides, as she'd told her tearful parents, she had a plan. She'd take the test for her GED, and it would be just the same as if she'd spent her whole senior year trolling through Bel Air High with the offspring of the rich and powerful, without having had to actually endure the experience.

"Hey, did I tell you I'm going out with Audrey Birnbaum tonight?" Lydia asked, interrupting Esme's thoughts.

"Twice." She put a forefinger to her lips. "Shhh. Steven's ready."

Finally, the crowd was silent, and Esme swung her eyes to her boss, one of the most powerful men in Hollywood. As usual he'd dressed down, in jeans, a blue work shirt, and a baseball cap to cover his balding pate.

"Welcome to everyone, and everyone welcome. I'm Steven Goldhagen—and I'm producing this year's show. I'm glad you're part of my team. We've got a ton of work to do before Saturday night, but you wouldn't be here if I didn't think you could deliver. Each and every one of you, whether you're a gaffer or a best boy, a hairstylist or a dresser, a set painter or a special assistant to the producer, is important to this production."

"He's talking about us!" Lydia said excitedly.

"So, you know what you have to do. Don't plan on much sleep between now and the show. We'll start sound checks tomorrow, costumes on Wednesday, dry tech Thursday, dress on Friday, and show on Saturday. And this goes without saying—stay out of the swag room. That's for our celebrities. I know it's tempting but I don't have time for nonsense."

Esme knew about the swag room, where clothing and cosmetic companies, electronics companies, designers, shoe manufacturers—anyone who'd benefit from having a celebrity use their gear or even be thought to be using their gear— would donate a huge lot of their best merchandise as giveaways to the stars. Esme had heard that celebrities could go home with tens of thousands of dollars' worth of gear. Designer jeans, Wiis and Xboxes, vacation packages to Vegas—it was all there for the asking and the taking. The official name for a swag room was a "gift lounge," but the operative effect was the same. Whatever you called it, loot was what you left with.

"So that's about it," Steven continued. "Work hard, work out your own problems with the supervisors, and chill on the autograph and photo requests. I promise you a kick-ass wrap party when the show's over. See you at the Kodak."

Steven gave his crew the thumbs-up, and they responded with a cheer and a standing ovation. Clearly, the worker bees of Hollywood weren't used to being treated this well, and they really appreciated it.

"This is going to be fun," Lydia said. "Do you know what we're going to be doing?"

"I think we're on door duty to start, starting tomorrow," Esme replied.

Lydia raised her eyebrows. "What's that?"

"The show's at the Kodak Theatre in Hollywood. Same place they do *American Idol* finals and the Oscars and the Daytime Emmys. We'll be with security at the front door," Esme explained. "You can't get in or out unless you're on the list."

Lydia pushed her bangs out of her eyes. "Why would security need us with them?"

"I don't know—'cause we're cute?" Esme replied. "This is Hollywood. None of it makes sense."

"We can get our friends in, though, right?" Lydia asked. "I told Flipper he could stop by."

"Lydia! Not the first day."

Esme was emphatic. Sometimes she wondered how Lydia had been raised, how she got all these crazy ideas. Then she'd remember, and decided it all made sense.

Lydia sighed. "Okay, okay. Can you give me a ride back to school now?"

"Sure. Just let me go to the—"

"Esme. You're here."

Esme froze. She knew the voice before she saw him. Jonathan Goldhagen. She knew she shouldn't be surprised. This was his father's event, he was an up-and-coming indie movie star, and he'd be a presenter on Saturday night. She'd wondered if he'd be at the lunch, and couldn't decide whether she wanted him to be or not.

Her heart pounded. She was hopeless to stop it.

All she could manage for him was, "Hi."

"Hey. You got a couple of minutes? I'd like to talk."

Esme shook her head. "Gotta take Lydia back to—"

"I can wait," Lydia assured her. She rose, and hugged Jonathan hello and goodbye. "Meet me in the lobby," she told Esme. "Take your time. I'll wait."

Lydia didn't wait around for Esme to respond, but took off toward the main doors to the hotel behind most of the rest of the crowd, leaving Esme and Jonathan practically alone with the small army of hotel cleanup staff that was already at work on the aftermath of the luncheon.

Damn. Jonathan. Esme had to admit, he looked great. Almost six feet tall, with the rangy build of a tennis player, short brown hair, and a scruffy three days' growth of beard, he wore a battered pair of Levi's 505s and a white Lacoste tennis shirt. She'd selected her outfit carefully that morning, on the off chance that she'd see him. She wore a straight, tight black skirt that fell to just below her knees, and very high, strappy aqua high heels. Her silk shirt was aqua too. It had cost her nearly two hundred dollars at a boutique on Montana, and that was on a half-price sale. She wasn't used to spending big money on her clothes, and she still felt guilty about buying it. But when she saw Jonathan's eyes sweep over her appreciatively, she was thrilled that she'd spent the money.

"I hear you're back home." He slid into one of the vacant chairs that had been occupied a few minutes before by a Kelly, and motioned for Esme to join him. She shrugged, and did. Her glass was still on the table. She took a sip before she turned to him.

"Yeah." She knew she was monosyllabic. She didn't care.

"That's good for the girls. I talked to Diane before I came over here. She's happy that you're back. And she said the twins are bouncing off the walls with joy."

"I missed them," Esme admitted. "I'm glad they're happy."

He looked at her cockeyed. "Are you happy?"

"Does it matter?"

He regarded her thoughtfully. "To me? Yeah, it matters."

"I came back because I was thinking of Easton and Weston. They've had so much disruption in their life already. Me leaving? That was another disruption and I feel terrible about how selfish I was. Plus they're starting first grade. No ESL. They're going to need some help. That help is me."

"Look, Esme." Suddenly, Jonathan lifted one of his short sleeves. "Look at this. Remember when you did this? Remember what we had?"

Esme looked. There was the freehand tattoo that she'd put on Jonathan's bicep, a magnificent depiction of a Ferris wheel, inspired by the wheel at the far end of the Santa Monica Pier, which she could see from Jonathan's apartment on Ocean Avenue.

"It looks good. You taking good care of it?"

Jonathan shook his head. "I'm not showing it to you for your assessment. I want you to remember."

"I do remember. I remember the last time we were to-gether." Esme ran her fingers through her thick hair. This was hard. Very hard.

"At the coffee place in the Echo, you mean."

Esme nodded. It had been at La Verdad coffeehouse. Jonathan had shown up to see her; he was about the only gringo in the whole joint. "You asked me two questions that day. One was whether I'd come back to work for your parents."

"And you never let me ask the second question," Jonathan reminded her. "That's why I'm here now."

He seemed about to go on, but a couple of hotel workers pushing mops and chattering in Vietnamese stopped to mop around where they were sitting. He waited until they were done. Esme both longed and dreaded to hear what he'd say. As much as she didn't want to want him, she still did.

"This won't take long," he assured her when the workers were out of earshot. "The other thing I wanted to ask you that night was, do you think we could go out again? Start fresh? So maybe you'll be my date for the wrap party after the awards?"

Start fresh. Wouldn't it be great if such a thing was possible? But she and Jonathan would always have their history. The rich white boy–poor brown girl thing. The getting caught in bed by his stepmother—that had been one of the most embarrassing moments of Esme's life.

Now she gazed at the beautiful tattoo on Jonathan's arm, maybe her favorite one she'd ever done. But she wasn't the same girl who had done that tattoo, who'd had a crush on

54

Jonathan long before she'd ever admit to it. She was not the same girl who had been a nanny over the summer. She was making so much money doing freehand tats now—she was the talk of hip Hollywood. She had power, and she loved how that felt. Even her best friend, Jorge, had commented on it, and he had been dead set against her dropping out of school to pursue her art. But when she was with Jonathan, she felt that power evaporating.

"I miss you," Jonathan continued, his voice low. "So much."

She felt the lump in her throat as she started to speak. "I need more time."

"For what?" His pale blue eyes were a mix of hurt and surprise. "I'm not asking you to marry me. I just want to take you to dinner."

Esme felt so torn. She remembered Lydia was out in the lobby, waiting for her.

"I'll call you." She stood up. "That's the best I can do," she added.

Instead of being angry, which would have made it easier for Esme to push him even farther away, he smiled. "It's good enough for me. I'd say we're making progress."

"And I'd say I've got to take Lydia back to school."

With those words, she fled, but stopped for a brief moment at the door to look back, to see if he was watching her. He smiled, poured himself a glass of pinot, and, in a silent salute, lifted it and drank.

Damn him. Did he have to be *that* fine?

6

"Holy shit, that's Audrey Birnbaum!"

"Audrey! Hey! Over here! I love your new single!"

"Audrey Birnbaum! Can you autograph my tits? Please?"

Flashes of light from cameras and cell phones lit the night as Lydia followed Audrey toward the Python Club on Melrose Avenue in West Hollywood, with Kiley trailing close behind. A long line of would-be partygoers snaked down the sidewalk behind a neon pink velvet rope, but Audrey clearly had no intention of waiting her turn. Instead, Lydia watched with admiration as Audrey ducked under that rope by the door and blew a kiss to the photographers before a beefy bouncer waved the three of them inside, through the club's double brass doors adorned with a swirling design of naked bodies.

Lydia had planned carefully for the night. She wore an orange and white Romeo and Juliet Couture sundress with a Sew What? crocheted cropped sweater, both of which she'd found in Kat's closet. Kiley had gone more low-key, in jeans and a sleeveless blue blouse. Her hair was up in its habitual ponytail, and the only makeup Lydia could see on her face was a swipe of lip gloss. As for the star of the show—Lydia was under no delusions: it was because of Audrey that they were able to bypass the masses and the cashier inside—Audrey wore a green Imitation of Christ miniskirt, a vest with nothing underneath it, and four-thousand-dollar Prada gladiator sandals Lydia had seen in *Vogue*. Her many tattoos were visible; Lydia reminded herself to tell Audrey about Esme's extraordinary freehand skills with the tattoo needle. Maybe she'd want another one, though Lydia couldn't imagine where she might fit it.

"Bloody pops," Audrey muttered as they headed down a dark corridor lit only with recessed purple black lights.

"What's a pop?" Kiley asked.

"Paparazzi," Audrey explained. "Vultures. Everywhere I go. I have no privacy."

"But if you had privacy you wouldn't be famous," Lydia reasoned. "And you love being famous, right?"

"Don't want to talk about it, sweets," Audrey insisted.

Lydia turned to Kiley—they shared a shrug as Audrey tugged them toward the main room of the club. Kiley rolled her eyes, which made Lydia roll her eyes right back. It had taken a lot of work to talk Kiley into coming out with them. All she wanted to do was sit in her guesthouse and moon over Tom and how they'd agreed to see other people while he was in Russia, which wasn't really what Kiley wanted at all.

Honestly. When it came to boys, Kiley had the sense of a bonobo.

Dance music throbbed from the balcony above the main room, whose walls were lined in faux snakeskin. Round red-lacquered candlelit tables dotted the space in a twisting arrangement of intimate seating areas. Three cages hung suspended from the ceiling. Inside each one, a hot, sweaty, nearly naked guy rocked out to the beat.

"You been here before?" Audrey yelled over the music.

Lydia and Kiley both shook their heads.

Audrey chucked her chin toward the cages. "Those are the Hot Dog Boys."

"I read about them!" Lydia exclaimed.

She had, back in the Amazon, in an air-dropped copy of *InStyle*. The Hot Dog Boys were the male equivalent of the Pussycat Dolls, and the auditions to become one were just as rigorous. Each guy had separate billing: Plumper, Meatier, and Juicier. Lydia wondered if they came with relish and mustard.

Audrey swept her hand toward the stage. "You'll see. They do a big show at midnight. My label just signed 'em. They look good, they dance their asses off, and they really can sing."

"They don't mind dancing in cages?" Kiley asked.

Audrey didn't answer, but from looking at them it was pretty clear to Lydia that they didn't mind at all.

Suddenly, a middle-aged guy in jeans and a Rolling Stones T-shirt materialized in front of them. He had thinning hair and the hard arms of someone who found his way to the gym on a regular basis. "Ms. Birnbaum, what an honor. Seymour Simon, I own this place."

"With P. and Ashton," Audrey filled in. "I know."

"Can I escort you and your friends to the VIP room? Stay out here, you'll be mobbed. You and your lady friends want to dance, let me know. I'll call Rodney or one of the other security guys."

Audrey nodded. "Lead the way. Bring us some Taittinger, love. And keep it coming."

"My pleasure."

The VIP room was upstairs, and enclosed in glass with heavy python-print drapes. At the moment the drapes were open, which allowed ordinary club attendees to gawk at the celebrities inside. Simon showed them in, and Lydia immediately picked out some of young Hollywood's biggest names hanging out on massive pillows in various animal prints, or sitting at low black tables that held plates of food. There were caviar and toast points, prawns wrapped in bacon, Kobe beef satay on a stick, and several kinds of sushi and sashimi. Half a dozen other people were talking, laughing, or dancing. A supermodel known for her *Sports Illustrated* cover was smoking a joint with a guy Lydia didn't recognize.

"Food!" Audrey yelped happily. They settled down behind a table, and Audrey immediately reached for some of the sashimi. "Then we'll do some lines. It's the only thing that gets me to stop eating."

She happily filled her plate with an array of food, and then excused herself to go say hi to that girl from *Juno*. From what Lydia could hear of the conversation, Audrey had invited her backstage at some concert in San Francisco, and they had bonded like sisters.

Lydia grinned. This was the life to which she could easily become accustomed.

She felt Kiley nudge her. "By lines, did she mean cocaine?"

"Don't know. I guess we'll find out." Lydia tried a piece of tuna sushi. It was the best she'd ever tasted. Not that it could compare to a peacock bass she'd caught and cleaned herself, but still.

"You aren't going to . . ." Kiley's worried voice trailed off.

"Kiley. Think. I've got powders and potions that'll make whatever she's got look like talcum powder, remember. I'm not even tempted by plain ol' coca leaves. Though there were plenty of times in the rain forest when we'd use it. It's real good for altitude sickness."

Audrey bopped back over to them. "Ellen says that when we go dance, we gotta get her." She tasted one of the crackers covered with caviar and nodded approvingly. "Decent. But it's better in Russia."

Two gorgeous guys entered the private room and made a beeline for them. One Lydia recognized—Payton Jeffries, bald and tattooed, was the lead singer of Clone, a neopunk band with a huge following. The other guy, tall and model handsome, with dark, spiky hair and broad shoulders, Lydia didn't recognize. He was hot, though. She wouldn't mind getting to know him.

"Audrey B!" Payton exclaimed happily. "I heard you were in town. Singing at the RMAs, right?" He wrapped Audrey in a bear hug.

"With Platinum," Audrey confirmed, then slung her arms around Lydia and Kiley. Lydia was thrilled, and grinned wildly. Payton introduced the hot guy with him as Matt Kingsley. Matt rubbed his square chin and pointed a finger at Kiley.

"I know you from somewhere."

"I doubt it," Kiley said.

"No, seriously, I do. Weren't you at Chris Martin's birthday party in Malibu?"

"Chris Martin—like, Coldplay Chris Martin?" Kiley laughed. "Hardly."

He folded his arms. "Well, I *do* know you."

The five of them sat around and ate, and polished off two bottles of champagne. Mostly, Payton and Audrey talked about the upcoming awards. Payton's new album was up for Album of the Year; his band would also be performing. When the second bottle of champagne was gone, he motioned to the waiter to close the heavy drapes to give them some privacy. When the curtains were closed, he took a vial of coke from his pocket.

"That's probably not a good idea," Kiley cautioned.

"For them, maybe," Audrey said, indicating the people on the other side of the curtain. "In here, nothing is illegal, sweets."

Kiley didn't look convinced. "I just went through Platinum's trial with her, and she nearly lost her kids over drugs. I'm sorry, but if you do that, I have to leave."

"Every party loves a pooper, that's why we invited you, party pooper!" Audrey sang. "We'll go to the ladies', where we can get fucked up in private." She stood up and held out a hand to Lydia. "You coming?"

Lydia couldn't help it—a little thrill ran through her. Not because she was attracted to Audrey; the girl thing just did not appeal to her. But Audrey was a superstar. She could party with anyone. And the person she had picked to hang out with was Lydia. On the other hand, Kiley looked kind of panicked. Lydia didn't want her friend to get all upset. But she didn't feel as though she should have to babysit Kiley, either.

Lydia's fingers entwined with Audrey's. "Sure," she said. "I'd love to come."

"I wish I had a place where I could do this all the time," Audrey groused. "I'm staying at the Four Seasons. They have, like, coke police there."

"I've got a big mansion to myself," Lydia told her.

"You do? How?"

"My aunt's in San Francisco, it's her place. And I promise, I'm not the cocaine police. In fact, I've got some powder from the jungle in Brazil that'll make you forget all about coke."

Audrey's eyes shone. "You do?"

"Sure. You want to check it out?"

"Shit," Audrey exclaimed. "I'll fucking move in!"

"Done deal. I've got the guesthouse, you can have the main house," Lydia offered.

"You're on."

Shit. She was serious. How cool was that? Hey, it would be an adventure. And if there was one thing Lydia loved, it was an adventure.

Someone opened the drapes again, and Kiley peered out at the faces looking in. Black, white, Latino, they were uniformly young and hip. Many of them glistened with sweat from the dancing going on downstairs. Sure, they were gorgeous, but Kiley didn't care. She was alone now—the others were in the bathroom doing who knew what, except for Matt, who had gone over to the bar for a cocktail. She twirled the straw in her Diet Coke. She didn't want champagne, or any of the great-looking food set out on the tables. She wasn't even in the mood to be here anymore. In fact, she was sorry she'd let Lydia talk her into coming.

All she could think about was Tom. His flight had already landed in Moscow, she figured. She checked her utilitarian Timex. It was just after ten here in Los Angeles, and it was eleven hours later in Moscow. That made it just after nine in the morning. Was Tom asleep? Or was he in some café with

Chloë Sevigny? Would they have dinner together tonight? What about Jessica Simpson? She imagined the three of them laughing and drinking vodka, with all these Muscovites coming up and asking for autographs.

She sighed. She did not want to be one of those girls who obsessed about her boyfriend all the time: was he cheating, did he want to cheat? It was so demeaning. She had hoped that between taking care of the kids and going to her new high school, she wouldn't have time to worry about Tom. But he'd only been gone for less than one day, and already she knew that no matter what she was doing or whom she was with, she was going to obsess. That was just the way it would be.

How long was the shoot again?

"Hey."

Matt came back, carrying another Diet Coke and a shot of tequila. "Don Julio. Tequila of the gods."

He set both down on the table and rejoined her. "Which would you like?"

"I'll do the Diet Coke."

"Then I'm the tequila." He rapped the shot glass on the table, then raised it to Kiley. "To my new friend in her too-cool jeans." He drank the whole shot, then wiped one finger across his lips. "Ahh. That could turn anyone into an alcoholic." He snapped his fingers. "I'm ready to hang with the lowlifes. Wanna go downstairs and dance?"

Kiley thought for a moment. She kinda did, but she knew that Lydia would never find her. And she was the one who had given Lydia a ride over here.

"Oh. No, thanks. But you go if you want to."

"Nah." He stretched, his biceps bulging out of his baby blue Wallflowers T-shirt. "Let's just hang. What do you do, Kiley? Singer? Actress?"

"Student," Kiley filled in.

"Oh, cool. USC? UCLA? Pepperdine?" Matt prompted.

"Someplace smaller." Kiley wasn't ready to admit to this guy that she was still in high school. "I'm also a nanny for Platinum's kids. You know, the rock star?"

Matt snapped his fingers again. "That's it. Her trial. You were involved."

"Against my will."

Matt laughed, smeared some caviar on a toast point, and topped it with a dollop of sour cream. "Yeah. I read the story in that tabloid. Couldn't have been fun for you. But it did great things for her career." He popped the caviar into his mouth and washed it down with some champagne. "Last album? Didn't even go gold. After the trial, it zoomed up the charts. What a world, huh?"

"What a world," Kiley agreed.

"Can I ask you something about that?" Matt plunged on without waiting for Kiley to respond. "Was she guilty? Because from what I read and saw, she was guilty as hell. Isn't that what the judge said before they lost the evidence?"

Kiley put a finger to her lips. "I'd really rather not talk about it, if you don't mind. I mean, she's my boss."

"Smart girl." Matt grinned at her.

"What about you? Are you a singer?"

"Can't carry a tune in a bucket," he admitted cheerfully, then reached for a piece of the octopus sashimi. Kiley had tried it before and found it a bit chewy, but Matt seemed to relish it. "What I really love is the beach—anything having to do with the ocean—"

"Me too," Kiley exclaimed. "Actually, anything under the ocean."

"You scuba?"

"I'm learning." Kiley shifted back onto her pillow and started to relax. She liked this guy. It was fine to talk with him. Wasn't it?

"Well then, we have something in common. The other thing I'm crazed for is photography. Wish I could make my living at that. I'm taking classes at Santa Monica College."

Kiley smiled. What a nice guy. "You're a student, too."

"Part-time. I pay the bills by modeling."

"My boyfriend's a model," Kiley said, and then immediately second-guessed herself. If she and Tom weren't exclusive, could she still call him her boyfriend?

"I've got it!" Matt Kingsley cried, snapping his fingers again. It was a cute habit. "I don't know you from the trial. I know you from Marym's birthday party up in Malibu. You were there with Tom Chappelle."

Marym was a stunningly beautiful Israeli model and a good friend of Tom's. He'd taken Kiley to the model's Malibu beach house for her birthday party. Even then, Kiley had felt insecure and jealous, certain that Tom and Marym had wanted to hook up.

Jeez, what was *wrong* with her?

"That was me," Kiley admitted. "Great party."

"It was, yeah. So . . . you and Tom have a thing going on, huh?"

66

"He left for Russia this morning. To shoot his new movie, *Kremlin Cowgirl*."

"We did a project together last week for Zac Posen," Matt said. "Tom was really jazzed about the movie. Hey, did you know that Marym is going to be in Russia for part of the shoot?"

No. Kiley had not heard that. "What?"

"Yeah, crazy coincidence, huh? Marym's shooting a *Vogue Italia* cover there next week. I'm sure Tom told you all about it."

"Oh, sure. I don't mind. It's cool."

She hated herself for lying—she prided herself on being an honest person—but she couldn't bear to admit that the guy she loved was most likely going to see his former girlfriend, *who just happened to be one of the top models in the world,* in Russia. And he hadn't bothered to mention it to Kiley.

"Great. It's cool that it's cool. Sure you don't want to head down to dance?"

Why the hell not? It certainly didn't do her any good to sit up here in the VIP hothouse obsessed about Tom and the Israeli bombshell doing the wild thing in the middle of Red Square.

The music from downstairs was piped into the VIP lounge. Lily Allen's voice came through the sound system. Lydia would be able to find her.

Matt rose, reached out a hand for Kiley, and helped her to her feet. He held her hand all the way down the spiral staircase that led to the packed dance floor. But when he put his arms around her waist to dance, it didn't feel as if he was hitting on her. She just relaxed and swayed to the music with him.

"So, where is it you do go to school?" he asked, after they'd danced for a while in comfortable silence.

"You have to promise not to laugh."

He took one hand from her waist and raised a palm. "On my grandmother's life—and my grandmother rocks."

"Okay, then. I'm still in high school."

"High school," he repeated.

"High school. I'm a senior. At Bel Air High."

Okay. She'd said it. And the floor had not opened up and swallowed her whole.

"Not laughing," Matt said, although he looked as if he wanted to. "So you're what—eighteen?"

"Seventeen. Eighteen in a month."

"Your secret is safe with me," he assured her, slipping his hand around her waist again. "We should hang out sometime," he added casually. "Go to the beach."

She stiffened, and he seemed to read her mind. "Hold on. I know Tom's your guy. But that doesn't mean we can't be buds. Like Tom and Marym. Right?"

"Right,"she agreed.

But even as she said it, her mind was not on hanging out with Matt at all. It was back on Tom and Marym in Red Square—outside Lenin's Tomb, to be precise. Walking hand in hand.

In some ways, that vision in her mind's eye hurt even more than imagining the two of them in the clinch.

Kiley let herself into her guesthouse, kicked off her Cons, and padded into the bedroom where she kept her laptop. She'd ended up having fun with Matt. They'd even made a date to go to the beach on Saturday. He was easy to talk to and comfortable to hang out with. That was good, since Lydia had spent the whole night practically superglued to Audrey. When Kiley had briefly gotten Lydia alone, she'd asked if Lydia was doing drugs. Lydia had laughed and reminded Kiley that she did not need to imbibe any local pharmaceuticals because she had her own, which were vastly superior, and besides, she didn't believe in using them for recreational purposes. As for giving some to Audrey, though, that was another story.

So, okay, maybe Lydia wasn't doing drugs. But it was clear to Kiley that hanging out with someone as famous as Audrey was its own kind of drug to Lydia, who was loving every minute of it. She got confirmation of that feeling when Lydia told her that Audrey was going to be her houseguest for RMA week.

"Do you have to ask Kat?" Kiley wondered.

"Don't ask, don't tell" was Lydia's response.

She grabbed her laptop from the desk and sat cross-legged on her bed to check her e-mail. Surely there would be something from Tom. Her eyes flicked down the list of messages. Spam, spam, and spam. Something from Esme about the schedule for the Rock Music Awards. Something from her best friend back in La Crosse.

Nothing from Russia. Nothing at all.

Well, it wasn't as if she couldn't reach out to him herself. What difference did it make who was in touch first? She put in his Gmail address and began to type:

Hi Tom—
Hope your flight was great and that you're over your jet lag. I've been trying to picture you there in Russia but honestly I can't imagine what it's really like, so please send me lots of pix.

Everything here is fine. I went to the Python Club
tonight with Lydia and her new best friend, Audrey
Birnbaum. Yes, that Audrey Birnbaum. It was fun.

Well, it's late so I think I'll hit the hay. I miss you
and think about you all the time—

Kiley frowned. *I miss you and think about you all the time*? It
was true, but that didn't mean she should say it. She erased
the line and instead added: *I miss you and think about you*.
Then she nibbled on her lower lip, trying to decide how to
sign off. Love? Hugs and Kisses? Sincerely?

Nothing seemed right. So she just signed her name and hit
Send before she could chicken out.

After she brushed her teeth, washed her face, and crawled
into bed, she found she couldn't sleep. Something was bother-
ing her. A lot. After waiting all these years when it seemed as
though everyone else was already having sex, she'd finally
found the One. Even then, she'd waited before making love
with him. When they'd finally done it, it had been so perfect—
like every dream she'd ever had about it, and then some.

But—what did it say about your relationship with the One
when you didn't even feel secure enough to write "Love" on
your e-mail to him?

Whatever it was, it couldn't possibly be good.

8

"Thank you, thank you. I just love it!"

"My pleasure," Esme told Luanna Venice, an entertainment lawyer who had just sat perfectly still for nearly two hours while Esme created one of her patented freehand tattoos just above Luanna's right ankle. Luanna had asked for a depiction of the scales of justice, but with that special Esme touch. Esme had done the scales in an outline of black and white, but then had added books to one of the scales, and, knowing Luanna had recently had a baby, a family holding hands to the other.

"What do I owe you?" Luanna asked. "I know you had to change your schedule to fit me in."

Luanna had lustrous streaky gold hair, which she shook with a carefree, too-well-practiced gesture. If she wasn't a lawyer, Esme thought, Luanna could have been a model. It was just so Hollywood—to look like you were playing a lawyer on TV instead of actually being one.

Entertainment lawyers made a mint, that much Esme knew. Unlike, say, her friend Jorge's father, Roberto, who had chosen to do public interest law, which meant he was never going to make anything close to a mint. Jorge was determined to follow in his father's footsteps.

"It's a thousand," Esme said matter-of-factly, even though the idea of someone dropping a thousand bucks for a tattoo was still a bit shocking to her.

Luanna was already reaching into her huge designer bag. "Great. Cash is okay?"

"Cash is fine."

"So here you go." Luanna counted out bills with a well-manicured right hand. "Ten hundreds, and two more for you. I can't wait for my friends to see this."

"You remember how to care for it, until it heals?" Esme asked nonchalantly, as if she received two-hundred-dollar tips every day.

Luanna grinned and tapped her bag. "I've got your information sheet, it's also up on your Web site, and you made me repeat it two times. I'd say I'm covered."

"Infection is bad for business," Esme pointed out. "I haven't had one yet."

Luanna laughed. "Well, I don't plan to be your first. Just give me a dozen of your business cards and get ready for your phone to ring."

Esme pointed Luanna to a small table in one of the two tattoo-application rooms she'd put into this office space. On that table was literature about her business and a stack of business cards. The whole thing still seemed unreal—that after years of doing tattoos either in her parents' house in the

Echo or just taking her equipment with her, she had rented actual office space, signed an actual lease, and opened up an actual business that had a phone number of its own and a listing in the business directory downstairs. "Esme Ink" is what she called it; she and Jorge had dreamt the name up together, enjoying the play on words. If it wasn't for Jorge, Esme wouldn't have any of this. He had already turned eighteen, and could legally sign paperwork that Esme, who was still a couple of months shy of eighteen, could not.

The office itself was fairly spartan. There was a tiny waiting area with two chairs, a coffee table, and some art books to inspire potential customers. There were two rooms for tattoos, since the office had formerly been a dentist's office, and two dentists had shared the space. Esme was using only one of the tattoo rooms at present, and had some vague thoughts about maybe subletting the space to another artist. But this whole project had come together so quickly that there'd been no time even to pursue that notion. Just getting up and running was complicated enough. There were licenses to apply for, inspections to secure, and then, there was the actual time of being at the shop. All the work wasn't even close to being finished. In fact, Jorge was supposed to arrive at any time with some sort of addendum clause to the lease that he wanted the landlord to sign.

Her parents were also supposed to stop by later. This was one of their rare days off from the Goldhagens. They were going to visit some friends of theirs from Mexico who worked downtown at a clothing manufacturing company, and then come to Century City to see Esme's new place of business.

It would be good to have Jorge on hand, she thought. Her

parents, Alberto and Estella—especially her mother—had been dead set against her leaving school to start her own business, even after she promised to get her GED. They did not work as hard as they did for her to be a high school dropout, they'd told her. She was such a smart girl, she'd gotten excellent grades, she would get a scholarship and be the first person in their family to go to college. How could she throw all of that away?

Esme felt a gnawing of guilt in the pit of her stomach. For the zillionth time she questioned the decision she'd made. She was letting her parents down. But opportunity had knocked, and she couldn't turn it away. At the rate she was going, by the time she was twenty-one, instead of graduating from college, she'd have enough money saved to buy her parents a fabulous house far, far away from Echo Park. Then, she told herself, they would finally appreciate the choice she had made.

Anyway, her parents loved Jorge. Maybe having him here when they showed up would deflect some of the criticism that was inevitably coming her way.

Once Luanna had the cards, Esme walked her to the front door of her studio. It was two-fifteen, which meant she had a few hours before she had to go back to the Goldhagens' to take the twins swimming. After that, she was to meet Steven at the Kodak Theatre, where the performers for the Rock Music Awards were rehearsing, to go over exactly what Esme, Lydia, and Kiley would be doing to help out.

"Thanks again," Luanna said, smoothing a nonexistent wrinkle from her yellow pin-tucked Michael Kors shirt. "I definitely will send some people your way."

"Great," Esme replied with a smile. "It was a pleasure to

meet you. I hope you love your tattoo." She had the post-tattoo gab down cold. Would Luanna come through with some referrals? Who knew? But it made sense to be polite to everyone. You couldn't charge what she charged and be a surly bitch. Esme had learned that in show business, everyone acted as if they were your best friends, even though tomorrow they wouldn't remember your name.

No sooner had Esme shown Luanna out, and deposited the twelve hundred dollars in a wall safe Jorge had insisted she install, that there were three quick rings on her buzzer telling her Jorge was downstairs at the locked glass door. She buzzed him through, then checked herself in the small waiting-room mirror—she wore a sleeveless red ruffled silk top with a cinched elastic waist, tight jeans, and high, strappy sandals from a boutique on Melrose. No more shopping at the "All Shoes $9.99" store in the Echo for her. She went to let her friend in.

He bounded out of the elevator wearing a backpack—Esme knew it had to be weighty with textbooks—and carrying a laptop computer in a black case. He wore black jeans and a black T-shirt under an open red shirt, and there was a grin spread across his face. He'd recently had his hair trimmed, Esme noted. He looked good. On the skinny side, yes, but there were muscles under that shirt, she knew. He wasn't nearly as tall as Jonathan, nor as traditionally handsome, and yet somehow he managed to be a chick magnet—her girlfriends were always hitting on Jorge.

"Here for a tattoo?" she joshed.

"No ink on this skin, *chica*. No tats is the new cool."

"I hope you're wrong—that would put me out of business." She opened the door; he followed her inside. "How's college?"

Jorge was a year ahead of her in school, and had started his freshman year on a full-ride academic scholarship at UCLA.

"College is to high school as a fresh peach straight off the tree is to ten-year-old canned fruit. I think I had that question on my SAT," he joked.

"So you love it," Esme translated.

"I do," he replied. "I'm taking an Eastern philosophy class, which is amazing. Great professor. Studied with the Dalai Lama. I'm planning a trip to Tibet next summer."

"You didn't tell me that."

"You've been kind of preoccupied with your own *la vida loca,*" he pointed out.

That was true, and she felt guilty about it. Here Jorge was, helping her every step of the way even though he, too, had been dead set against her dropping out of school, and she had spent zero time asking about what was going on in his life.

That's going to change, Esme vowed. "You want coffee?"

He plopped down onto one of the bright orange plastic chairs in the waiting room. "Yeah. Also, half of what you made today."

"Oh, you shakin' me down now?" Esme teased as she poured a cup and handed it to him. She had a coffee station set up for customers, and a small plate of fancy cookies that no one ever touched.

Esme slid into a chair next to Jorge. "Okay, so tell me all about you."

He sipped the hot coffee carefully. "What, now I'm supposed to make up for lost time?"

"Seriously," Esme insisted. "I want to know."

"Okay. The Latin Kings are doing a benefit for the SAJE—"

"What's that?"

Jorge shook his head. "You haven't been away from the hood for *that* long. Strategic Actions for a Just Economy. All these yuppies are moving into the old neighborhood, driving up rents, driving our people out of their homes."

"Why would some rich gringos want to live in the Echo?" Esme wondered. "I don't get it."

"Oh, maybe you didn't hear. The Echo is hip now," Jorge said archly. He took a paper out of his backpack and handed it to Esme. "Your new sublet clause. You're safe if you want to share the space."

"Thanks. What would I do without you?"

"I often ask myself that. When're your parents coming?"

As if in answer to that question, the buzzer sounded again, long and insistent, as if the person trying to get in was in a terrible hurry.

"Gee, you wouldn't think they'd be so eager to get up here," Esme muttered. She was really not looking forward to having her parents there. She went to the intercom and pressed Talk.

"Yes?" she asked.

"Esme!" her father cried. He sounded breathless. "Let us in! Hurry!"

Esme pressed the button to unlock the door downstairs and traded a look with Jorge. Whatever was up couldn't possibly be good.

Two hours later, a pale-faced Esme was sitting with her parents and Diane Goldhagen in Steven's home office. The twins were up in their bedrooms playing with their state-of-the-art dollhouses; their swimming lesson had been canceled. Steven was on his way from the Kodak Theatre so that he could be part of this meeting.

Esme looked at her parents, who sat together on the edge of the couch, both of them stiff with fright. Her father wore black trousers and a short-sleeved light blue shirt; her mother an embroidered full skirt and a pretty red blouse. It occurred to Esme that this was probably the first time they'd been on the Goldhagens' estate not wearing their work uniforms.

"Steven will know what to do," Diane reassured them.

Esme hoped she was right. She turned to Jorge. "Did you call your father again?"

"Texted him. He's in court all day. He——"

Steven stepped into the room. He wore baggy jeans and a white tennis shirt, his trademark baseball cap planted firmly on his head. "Okay, everyone stay calm. Tell me the whole story. All Diane said on the phone was 'There's an emergency with Esme's parents, come home.' So . . . I'm home." He sat on the camel suede high-backed chair and waited.

With that, Esme's parents started babbling in a mix of broken English and Spanish—when they got nervous, their English got much worse. But a few words from Jorge made them stop, and then her friend turned to her. "Esme, why don't you explain to the Goldhagens what your parents told us?"

Esme saw the pain in her parents' eyes as she started to speak. "My folks went down to Consolidated Threads to visit friends who work there. You know it? It's this clothes manufacturer downtown."

Diane nodded. "I know Consolidated. Steven, I think Ernie Edelson's ex-father-in-law inherited it from his parents. You know Ernie. From the synagogue."

Steven nodded. "Yeah. Go on, Esme."

She glanced at her parents, who now had joined hands. Those hands were clenched together so tightly that they were almost white. "So here's the thing," Esme continued. "Consolidated is using undocumented immigrant laborers to do their sewing. Lots of them."

"So what?" Diane asked. "Everyone uses undocumented laborers. We use undocumented workers. We don't care about silly papers." Diane fixed her eyes on Alberto and Estella. "You've been working for us for three years. I don't understand why this situation is so dangerous for you two. What difference does it make?"

Jorge cleared his throat. "It makes a difference to Homeland Security, Mrs. Goldhagen."

"Diane."

"Diane, thank you. It makes a difference to the Department of Homeland Security. This afternoon, they raided Consolidated. Big raid. I imagine it'll be on the news," Jorge related.

"Many arrested," Estella added.

"It's like this, Diane. There were all these Homeland Security guys there. They were checking everyone. It didn't matter if you worked there or not. My parents, they don't have papers. They got in line with everyone else; they had to, they weren't allowed to leave. But when the Feds came in, a lot of people ran. It was chaos, running, police with clubs. My parents got away. They came right to me."

"Fotografía, Esme. ¡No olvidáte las fotografías!" Esme's father implored her in Spanish.

"There were photographers there," Esme translated. "My parents believe they were photographed."

"And that the cops are coming after them," Jorge added.

"*Sí.*" Esme's father nodded.

Steven tapped a forefinger thoughtfully against his lips. "That must have been very frightening. To see your friends taken by the police, to be lined up and asked for their papers. I can't imagine what it would be like. I have never had an experience like it in my life, although my grandparents did, back in Poland. Diane and I can't blame you for running away. Do we, Diane?"

"Not at all," Diane insisted. "Not in the least."

"I know the natural inclination is to worry," Steven continued. "I would worry if I were you. But my instincts are telling me they were looking to punish this company for hiring a lot of illegal workers. They weren't looking for just the two of you, even if they put you in the line. Did you ever get asked for your name and address?"

"They were asking everyone in the line but they didn't get to us," Estella said.

"Good," Steven said. "Then I think you'll be safe. Just in case, I can put in a call to a friend of mine at the United States Attorney's office. They'd be handling this."

Esme felt relief wash over her. "That would be wonderful; thank you so much."

Her parents nodded.

"Just go do it, Steven," Diane urged her husband.

"I'll do it now."

Esme felt like crying. She was born in America, which made her a citizen. Not so for her parents. They tried to lie low, do their off-the-books work, and just live their lives. If Steven could assure them that nothing would change, that would

80

mean the world to her and her family. She said a silent prayer of thanks that she had had the good judgment to come back here to work, that the Goldhagens were such decent people.

Steven went to his BlackBerry, picked out a phone number, and made a call—he asked for Barry Barrett at the United States Attorney's office. When whoever answered the phone heard the name Steven Goldhagen, the call went through.

"Barry? Steven Goldhagen. How the hell are you? How's Mary? And the boys?"

Barry took quite a while to say how he was, apparently. Ditto for his family. It took five minutes before Steven could get to the meat of the matter.

"I heard about an immigration raid today at Consolidated—no, it doesn't affect me. Just that I've got some people on a project whose relatives were affected." Steven was smooth, Esme could say that for sure.

"Uh-huh. Uh-huh." Barry apparently had a lot more to say. "Uh-huh. Well, thanks. And say hi to Mary." He clicked off.

"Well?" Diane asked.

Steven sighed. "I'm afraid we have a problem on our hands. A very serious problem."

9

Lydia came down to the pool after a late lunch to find Audrey sunbathing on a hot pink bath towel, which nicely set off her now-golden skin. She was golden everywhere, Lydia noted. She could see everywhere because Audrey was stark naked. This didn't bother Lydia at all.

That's the way we did it in Amazonia. This is my kinda girl, she thought as she moved close enough to block the sunlight from reaching Audrey's eyes. She knew that she, Esme, and Kiley were all due at the Kodak Theatre at six for rehearsal. They'd be working as gofers, which meant their job was to do anything the producers or the stars wanted. She was looking forward to it. It would be fun. For now, though, she had a few hours of relaxing. She also had to read the first five chapters of *The Sun Also Rises* for English. Maybe she could just get Kiley to kind of summarize it for her. She wasn't about to take up her time with actually reading the book, not when there were so many more exciting things to do.

The night before, at the club, she'd offered her aunt's house to Audrey on the chance that the star might want to stay there during the days running up to the awards. There was plenty of room, and Lydia had to admit it was almost too quiet with her aunt and the kids away. So they'd driven straight from the club to Audrey's hotel, where the bell staff loaded five huge suitcases of clothes into their limo, and then driven to Kat's mansion. Lydia put Audrey in the guest room of the main house, showed her where everything was, and went to sleep in her guesthouse not believing her luck. One of the world's hottest rock stars was living at her house. How lucky could a girl from the jungle get?

Her face shaded, Audrey opened her eyes. "Good morning. Just getting up?"

"I've been up since eleven," Lydia admitted. She wore one of her favorite bikinis—orange and pink paisley—and sun-glasses on her head held back her bangs. Wanting to make sure that Audrey felt at home, she casually took off the top of her bikini and then settled onto the chaise next to Audrey's.

"Nice allover tan, sweets," Audrey commented.

"Bathing suits aren't really big in the rain forest. I remember when a doctor from New Jersey came in by boat wearing an orange Speedo. The witch doctor couldn't stop laughing for a week. How'd you get your tan?"

One of those spray-on booths in Hollywood," Audrey admitted. "I'm usually more of an indoor-nighttime kind of girl." She lifted a martini glass filled with a pinkish drink. Next to her was a pitcher full of whatever it was she was drinking. "Cheers. Pomegranate martinis, courtesy of your aunt's cook."

"Paisley? She used to be totally crunchy before my aunt's wife left," Lydia said. "Nothing stronger than wheat-germ shakes got mixed in this house. But once Anya left—woo-hoo!"

Audrey sat up and poured herself another martini. "Want one?"

"I think I want to swim. It's hot."

"Don't you have school or something?" Audrey looked at her cockeyed. "Lord, I can't believe you're still in high school."

"I'm wise beyond my years," Lydia assured her. "I'm cutting." She bent her knees and scratched a mosquito bite on her thigh. "It's funny, because I used to just dream of going to an American high school. Now that I'm in one . . . big ol' yawn."

Audrey laughed. "I love you! You're so real. Everyone you meet in the music world is so fucking fake, you know?"

"It's not just the music world," Lydia said. "It's an L.A. thing. On the other hand, the glamour and the clothes and the clubs . . . big upside." She stood up and stretched. "Excuse me. The water calls."

Lydia dove into the crystal blue pool with barely a splash behind her. She loved to swim. Back in Brazil with her parents, living among the Amarakaire tribesmen, swimming was one of the few things she could do that was exactly the same as it had been when she lived in America. Well, not exactly the same. She always had to make sure she didn't have any open cuts or scrapes when she dove into the Rio Negro, because piranhas tended to be drawn to blood. And she occasionally found herself looking into the eyes of a curious wild boar when she clambered back up on the bank. When she was cutting neatly through the water with her powerful crawl, though, swimming was liberating.

She swam for a long time, and stopped counting after sixty laps. Freestyle, breaststroke, even the butterfly. She did them all. After three final freestyle laps at top speed, aided by the flip turn she'd taught herself in the rain forest, she finally quit and held on to the side of the pool, breathing more easily than anyone who'd just swum that hard had a right to.

Audrey came over to her. She'd applied a fresh layer of sunblock to her flat abs; Lydia could tell from the streaks. "Do you know that you just did seventy-eight laps?"

"I wasn't counting," Lydia replied honestly.

"Gawd, I hate all sports," Audrey moaned. "The only way I want to sweat is horizontally with a bloke who strikes my fancy. Well, sometimes vertically," she amended. "Ever do it at the Hot Zone bar up against the stall in the loo?"

"Nope," Lydia replied, hoisting herself out of the water. "Sounds like an adventure."

"Definitely," Audrey agreed, sipping her drink. "You've had such an exotic life, ducks. What else did you do in the Amazon?"

"Fished. Hunted. Got homeschooled by Mom and Dad. Read every American fashion magazine I could get my hands on until they disintegrated."

"Not many designer shops to haunt?" Audrey asked.

"A plate in your lip is considered a fashion statement. Some of it was fun," Lydia mused. "I liked the shaman. He was cool. Awesome potions."

Audrey looked interested. "Tell me about them."

Lydia shrugged. "They had medicine there long before

the white doctors ever showed up. Herbal stuff, and lots of it worked better than anything the Western doctors ever thought up."

"God, I love that," Audrey trilled. "It's so back to nature!"

Lydia was flattered by Audrey's attention and enthusiasm, so she went on. "They had killer recreational stuff, too. There is nothing like a stoned Ama. Nothing."

She laughed at the memory of Ama men rolling around in the mud, totally flying from something the shaman had blown up their noses. She'd partaken once or twice, as part of special ceremonies, but never just as a lark. That shit was *powerful*.

Audrey's eyes shone. "Did you by any chance bring any of that stuff back?"

"Of course," Lydia replied.

"Let's give 'er a go," Audrey urged.

Lydia shook her head. "Those powders and potions are no joke. I've got one that can knock a person out until you think they're dead."

"I so need to give that to my ex—bloody bastard screwed one of my backup singers." She leaned toward Lydia. "Aw, come on. I've done everything there is to do and tried everything else I can find. It helps my creativity. No, really. It does. Come on. Let's get stoned the Ama way."

Lydia wanted to say no. On the other hand, she loved all the attention from Audrey, loved hanging out with a rock star.

She could let Audrey try something that wasn't too heavy or long-lasting, since they were due at the Kodak in the late afternoon, Audrey included. Lydia did have one potion, derived from a rare jungle root, that produced vivid hallucinations, but only for an hour or so. The Amas used it in religious ceremonies.

She described the powder to a practically salivating Audrey, but then added, "I don't want you to do it today, though."

"Why the bloody hell not?" Audrey asked, obviously irritated.

"In case you have a bad reaction. I don't want to be responsible for you missing your rehearsal tonight."

"Balls," Audrey spit.

"Another time, though, I promise," Lydia added quickly. "If you want, I can go get the blowguns and we can practice shooting at targets."

"Pass on the blowguns, I'm going to have another martini," Audrey declared. "And I want that powder *soon*." She poured herself another drink and then lay back down on her blanket, smiling approvingly. "The Hotel Lydia. Two thumbs up."

The stars were in the greenroom at the Kodak Theatre; the worker ants were milling around backstage and in the house. The sound equipment was set up onstage for the rehearsal, which was supposed to have begun a half hour ago, but they were still waiting for Steven Goldhagen to show up. Lydia sat with Kiley in the tenth row center, watching various workers onstage do whatever it was that needed doing.

"You think it's weird that Esme isn't here yet, either?" Kiley asked Lydia.

Lydia shrugged. "Got me, sweet pea." Her mind was still on her conversation with Audrey, who, at that moment, was in the greenroom with the other stars. "Let me ask you a hypothetical," Lydia began. "Hypothetically, would it be wrong for me to give Audrey some Ama dust just for fun?"

"Oh, Audrey, your new best friend," Kiley said, her voice flat.

"You'd love her if you got to know her," Lydia insisted. "She's fabulous. And she thinks I'm fabulous."

Kiley curled a stick of gum into her mouth. "You are fabulous. But doesn't it seem weird to you, how once you get here, she's in the greenroom and you're down here with the little people?"

Lydia thought about that. "Not really. Anyway, if Tom was here and he was going to be a presenter or something, he'd be in the greenroom and you'd be down here."

Kiley's face darkened. "Don't remind me. Anyway, in answer to your question, yes, I think it would be wrong for you to give Audrey some herbal drug so that she can party."

"It's not illegal," Lydia pointed out.

"Because the FDA never heard of it. What if she gets sick or something? It'll be your fault."

Lydia sighed. That was true. It was just so complicated.

Kiley checked her watch again. "I'm really starting to get worried."

Lydia knew there had been phone calls to Steven, because some flunky had made an announcement. Evidently all he'd said was that he'd be there as soon as he could. Lydia had tried to reach Esme, but got her voice mail.

"Yo, if I could have everyone's attention."

The crowd quieted and focused on a tall African American man who was onstage speaking into the mike. He had a shaved head and wore black jeans, a white T-shirt, and a black sport coat.

"For those of you who don't know me, I'm Alan Witherspoon, Steven's partner at Goldhagen Productions. I just got off the phone with Steven, who has asked us to go ahead with tonight's rehearsal while he tends to a family matter."

That announcement made even the normally unflappable Lydia a little nervous.

"Steven says everyone is healthy," Alan continued, "and he'll be back with us tomorrow. So everyone adjust your rehearsal by forty-five minutes, and let's get started."

Immediately people began running around, clearly with important things to do—not that Lydia had any idea what those things were. Esme was supposed to lead Lydia and Kiley in their duties, so they had no clue what they should be doing.

"Hey, are you two Lydia and Carol?" a thin young woman asked them. Her red ponytail stuck out the back of a black baseball cap.

"Lydia and Kiley," Lydia corrected, pointing to the name tags on their shirts.

"Whatever. I'm Jocelyn, one of the production coordinators. Alan told me you were sitting out here. You're supposed to be *working*."

"No one told us what to do," Kiley explained.

"Great," Jocelyn grunted. "I need you to—" The headphones draped around her shoulders crackled. "Hold on." She stepped away from Lydia and Kiley. "What?" she barked into the headphones.

Just then, Kiley's cell phone rang. She checked caller ID and saw with relief that it was Esme. She put the phone to her ear. "Esme? Where are you? Where's Steven? What's going on?"

"Put it on speaker," Lydia insisted. Kiley shook her head emphatically, then stepped several feet away to where she could evidently hear better. Lydia followed, but all she could understand was Kiley's repeated "I see, I understand, uh-uh, uh-uh, uh-huh." And then, finally, "If there's anything we can do, call us."

When Kiley clicked off, her face was ashen.

"What?" Lydia commanded.

"It's Esme's parents. They were almost caught in an immigration raid. And now Esme thinks that Homeland Security is after them."

"Shit on a stick," Lydia cursed. Now she was *really* worried for her friend.

"Esme's going back to Echo Park tonight with her parents," Kiley relayed. "They're going to meet with Jorge and his father, who's a big lawyer." The words were tumbling out of Kiley's mouth now. "Steven Goldhagen went downtown to talk to a friend of his who's with the government."

"So that's what's going on," Lydia muttered. Lord, Esme had to be going crazy. It was one thing to voluntarily leave your parents, as she had left hers, but quite another to have your parents forced out of the country forever.

"Why are you two still sitting here?" Jocelyn yelled at them, having finished whatever business she'd been attending to on her headphones. "You should be in the greenroom. They need you there right away." Her voice was high-pitched.

"We're there," Lydia assured her as she and Kiley moved into the aisle. "But just one little thing, Jocelyn? It never hurt anyone to be sweet. Especially to volunteers," she added, a smile on her face.

Jocelyn ignored the advice and thrust a list at Lydia. "On second thought, do this first. Take this. Do you drive?"

"I do, she doesn't," said Kiley.

Jocelyn spoke to Kiley. "These are food orders for the performers. Go to the Grove at Farmers Market, fill the orders, and be back in an hour. Here's money. Get receipts."

Kiley took the envelope filled with money. "But . . . there's all kinds of food in the greenroom," she pointed out.

"Well, that's not the food they want," Jocelyn replied. She turned to Lydia. "You. Come backstage with me. I've got a bunch of dogs for you to walk, and make sure you pick up their poop because I swear the paparazzi knows if a famous dog's poop doesn't get scooped, and then the star gets bad press. Paris's dog, Jessica's dog . . ."

"Not that I don't love pooches because I really do," Lydia drawled. "But don't they have their own people to do that?"

"Today you're 'their people,' " Jocelyn snapped. "Happy scooping." She hurried off.

"Hurricane Jocelyn," Lydia quipped.

Jocelyn whipped around from a hundred feet away. "I have super hearing. I heard that! *Go!*"

Kiley took off for the parking lot and Lydia headed backstage. Here she was, supposed to be all concerned about scooping up pampered-pooch poo, while her friend Esme was worried about something really important. What would it be like to have your parents facing deportation? She couldn't imagine, and didn't even want to imagine.

10

"Here we are. Lucky Strike Lanes in Hollywood," Matt announced as he held the door to the bowling alley open for Kiley. Next to the door was a giant neon blue bowling pin; inside that pin were Day-glo red and yellow letters that read BOWL HERE!

They entered the cool and dark bowling alley, which, Kiley noted, looked absolutely nothing like the Bowl-o-Rama back home in La Crosse. There were dozens of small high-top tables surrounded by square red leather chairs, most of which were taken by the young, the hip, and the beautiful. A thirty-foot bar was manned by guys who obviously doubled as male models. The forty or so lanes were backlit with the same neon blue as the sign outside, music videos running behind them as a backdrop. Audrey Birnbaum's latest hit pulsated through the sound system.

"Bowling is suddenly cool?" Kiley asked, raising her voice over Audrey's blaring one.

"It's been cool for the last five years. Actually, it's on the downswing. But still high enough on the hipness scale for us to show our faces. And this place? Coolness personified." Matt grinned and led Kiley toward the desk where a girl in low-slung white shorts and a blue bowling shirt with the name "Ashlee" embroidered in darker thread was handing out bowling shoes.

"That's trendy L.A. for you," Matt went on. "A couple of the beautiful people get photographed at a place like this; the next thing you know, it's the new place to be."

"Hey!" Kiley exclaimed, because Matt had just steered her right past the shoe desk. "Don't we need shoes?"

"Sure. Someone will get them for us. Come on."

Kiley shook her head. Someone else would get their bowling shoes? Now that was a new level of decadence, even by L.A. standards.

Matt led her to red leather double doors. "Right this way."

Kiley was confused. "I thought we were bowling."

"We are. With some friends."

They had entered what was clearly a private room, with four bowling lanes of its own. The couches were red velvet and retro-looking; the bowling balls were clear and filled with various colored stones, like a set of kids' marbles. Gorgeous young women were bringing people bowling shoes, food, and drinks—or, Kiley figured, pretty much anything their little overprivileged hearts desired.

"Is this the bowling version of a VIP room?" Kiley asked.

Matt led Kiley to one of the kidney-shaped sofas. "Yep. But tonight it's a private party room. Hey, Serinda, what's up?" He waved at an impossibly tall, impossibly gorgeous young woman with long, wavy raven hair who had just stepped over to one of the ball-return machines. The woman waved back, then reached for her bowling ball to take her turn.

"Who is that?" Kiley asked.

"Serinda Swan—new face of Guess watches—beat out Marym herself for that gig. It's a very big deal. Pays a mint." Then he cocked his head toward a blond girl, also impossibly tall, admirably thin, but more waiflike, with huge eyes. She was taking a tall orange-colored drink from an African American waitress in the same bowling shirt as Ashlee. "That's Lily Donaldson—she's on fire right now. The redhead about to roll in lane one? Abbey Lee. From Australia. Did Gucci for Fashion Week in New York. Went swimming in the fountain at Lincoln Center but no one took her picture. The guy she's holding hands with? Slade Wayne, also an Aussie. You might recognize him from that TV ad where a girl swims across a lagoon to get to him because he's holding a plate of wienies. Freud would have a field day with—"

"Hold on," Kiley interrupted. "I feel like I walked into a movie a half hour late. You asked me if I wanted to hang out and go bowling. I said sure. Now we're at some kind of bowling modeling convention."

"It's a party for Abbey and Slade," Matt explained. "They just got engaged."

Kiley was incredulous. "I'm at an engagement party for two people I don't even know?"

"Relax," Matt assured her. "This is a very casual thing for the L.A. friends. The official party is in the Hamptons next weekend. Total Jay Gatsby, including the white clothes. I wouldn't want to be there on a bet."

"I'm bound to run into people I met with Tom. This is just very awkward."

"I promise they won't think you're my date." Matt flashed his disarming grin. "If it helps, I could borrow a lipstick and write 'She Belongs to Tom Chappelle' on my forehead. You got lipstick?"

Kiley reddened. "I don't need—never mind. I know you were joking." She really needed to redirect this conversation. "What about you, Matt? Are you seeing anyone?"

He looked chagrined. "I'm a true romantic. And I'm suffering from an unrequited crush. It's a new concept in the realm of painful. Alas, I press on."

Kiley sympathized. "Those are the worst."

She tried to imagine what kind of girl would reject Matt. He was gorgeous, nice, friendly. It was hard to believe he couldn't get the girl he wanted. Some girls were just so incredibly picky.

Then she realized something. "Umm? Is your crush here? Is that why you brought me, because you're hoping to make her jealous?"

Matt hesitated. "Not exactly."

Kiley laughed. "Yes, exactly. Don't worry. I'm not offended. Although I think you could have brought someone a lot cuter than me if you were going for the jealousy thing. Which girl is it?"

Before Matt could answer, a perky blonde in the official blue bowling shirt approached them. "Hey, what size bowling shoes can I get you two?"

Matt turned to her. "Kiley? Ready to roll a few frames? Whatever you want to do is cool with me."

Kiley considered. It would be melodramatic to leave. There were tons of people in the room; it really did seem very casual. Besides, she knew what it was like to be into a guy you didn't think was into you back. Surely Tom was hanging out with big groups of beautiful people in Russia. She was probably overreacting.

She smiled at the young woman. "Size eight works."

"Ten and a half for me," Matt said. He also ordered them buffalo burgers and mango milk shakes before the girl moved off. Then he launched into a story about a recent audition, but Kiley was distracted because Heidi Klum and Seal had just walked in. Heidi wore skinny jeans and a white tank top; Seal was in a white seersucker suit. Kiley almost took a picture with her cell phone for Lydia, who would appreciate it much more than she did.

"Have you heard from Tom?" Matt asked. He reached for a handful of mixed nuts from the orange art deco bowl in the middle of the table.

"A couple texts," Kiley replied.

Both had been short and to the point, texts he could have sent to his cousin or to some casual acquaintance. *Hi, I'm fine, more soon,* that kind of thing. Not that she planned to share those details with Matt.

"Huh. Interesting. My friend Val heard from him yesterday."

"Who's he? Another model?"

"He's a she. A body double."

Kiley had no idea what he was talking about, but her stomach clenched at the mere idea that Tom had been in communication with another girl. She covered well, though. Or tried to. "She's a what?"

"You know. Body double for famous actresses. Like she'll be one star's legs for a legs close-up if the star has crap legs. She'll be another star's butt if that star doesn't want to show hers on camera. Same thing for sex scenes, et cetera, et cetera. It pays pretty well. Want some of these nuts?"

Kiley shook her head. Eating was out of the question. "So her legs and butt and breasts and everything in between must be rocking."

"Oh yeah," Matt agreed. "They are. Miss Rockin' Bod herself. I'm sure Tom told you about her. They used to hang out."

"Hang out or hook up?"

Matt's eyebrows rose. "Oh wow. That was a long time ago. Like months ago."

Kiley leaned forward and hoped her neediness wasn't bleeding through. "Which one was it?"

But instead of answering, Matt tugged Kiley to her feet. "Come on, relax. It was before you were ever in his life. Let me introduce you around. These people all know Tom. They'll be psyched to meet his girlfriend. You know lots of them already, I bet."

Kiley didn't want to be introduced. She wanted to know about Val and Tom, and why he'd been in touch with her—ohmigod, what if he'd actually called her?

"Kiley?"

"What?"

"You okay?" Matt asked.

He'd stopped and turned to her just outside a circle of laughing, chatting beautiful people he clearly wanted them to join. She felt like crying. *Why* was Tom talking to Val at all? Why hadn't he even mentioned her to Kiley? Now here she was, at this party with this guy—practically a random guy—and she didn't even want to be here.

She forced herself to calm down. It was a bowling alley, not a suite at the Hotel Bel-Air. So she slapped a smile on her face, assured Matt everything was fine, and moved forward to meet his beautiful friends.

"Hey, everyone!" Matt called out. "Come meet Tom's lady!"

Kiley was surprised to find the door to her guesthouse unlocked. That was odd. She was sure she'd locked it when she left. Hadn't she? Man, she was tired. Not that bowling two games (scoring a middling 118 both times—at least she was consistent) or making small talk with models and friends of models was all that strenuous. Or the fact that she'd momentarily been the center of attention when a bunch of people recognized her from Platinum's trial and the article about her in the *Universe*. None of that took very much energy. It was more her anxiety about Tom. She hated that she was obsessing about him.

She moved into the living room and automatically reached for the light switch, thinking that she really should get up early and put in a half hour of studying for the quiz in chemistry tomorrow—chemistry was definitely not her long suit—when she realized there was a lump on her couch under the pink and white quilt. A human lump. One small arm and one leg stuck out. The hand attached to the arm had black nail polish on it.

Serenity?

Kiley crouched down and tugged the quilt, revealing Serenity's glossy blond tresses. She smiled, remembering how, when she'd first met Serenity, the girl had refused to wash her hair. Ever. Now she cornered the market on upscale hair products. She washed it and blew it dry. How many other third-graders did that?

Kiley almost laughed. Here in Bel Air? Probably a lot. Serenity even had a friend the same age who had her hair done twice a week at her home salon, just like Mommy did.

Serenity burrowed into the quilt but opened her eyes. "Kiley."

"Hey, sweetie. How'd you get in my house?"

"It's Mom's house, you just live here," Serenity said in a sleepy voice. "I know where Mrs. Cleveland keeps the spare key."

Kiley kept stroking Serenity's hair, her tone as gentle as her hands. "That doesn't mean you can come in here without my permission. Is everything okay?"

Serenity sat up and rubbed her eyes. "There's this boy I like."

"And you wanted to talk to me about him?"

Serenity nodded. "But you weren't here and your door was locked. So I decided to wait for you." She leaned her head against Kiley's shoulder.

"We could have talked about this boy tomorrow," Kiley pointed out.

"But I couldn't sleep," Serenity complained, ignoring the

fact that Kiley had just found her very *much* asleep. "See, this boy in my class, Devon, well, I like him so much. But I don't know if he likes me back."

Kiley wanted to launch into the "you're too young for boys" lecture, but she knew it wouldn't do any good. Besides, she was glad that Serenity had confided in her.

"Like about two weeks ago I went up to him in the gym— everyone was playing dodgeball which is a stupid game—and I asked him if he wanted to hook up and he said yes," Serenity explained.

"Hook up" was such an ambiguous term, Kiley thought. It could mean anything from "let's hang out together" to "let's have hot monkey sex all night." Kiley sent up a quick prayer that in this case, Serenity was referring to the former and not the latter.

"Like you wanted to hang out with him," Kiley clarified.

"Duh. I wanted him to be my boyfriend. So he said yes. So then we went out—"

"Hold on," Kiley interrupted. "How could you go out? You're in grade school."

Serenity heaved a long-suffering sigh. "When you took me and my friend Molly to the Beverly Center we met up with Devon and Pistachio in the food court."

Kiley felt overwhelmed. "Pistachio is someone's name?"

"This other guy in my class who Molly likes, jeez! So I asked Devon if he wanted to make out but then his nanny came to get him—"

Kiley couldn't help herself. She interrupted Serenity again. "Serenity, you're too young to be making out."

"Yeah, whatever, maybe in *Wisconsin*. So then yesterday at

school I saw Devon holding hands with Simone—this other girl in my class who already has boobs. So I'm all like, 'But I thought you were my boyfriend' and Devon is all like, 'I am,' so why was he holding hands with Simone?"

"Sounds like maybe he's not ready to have just one girlfriend," Kiley mused.

"I guess." Serenity sat up and rubbed her eyes. "It makes me sad."

"I know the feeling," Kiley said. Funny. How different was her situation with Tom, really? She gave Serenity a quick hug. "You want me to walk you back to the house?"

"Can I sleep here just this once? Please-please-please?" Serenity wheedled.

"But your mom will worry when she sees your bed is empty."

"Are you on drugs? She won't wake up until way after I'm already at school."

Kiley knew that was true.

"Okay," she decided. "Just this once."

"Thanks." Serenity lay back down and Kiley tucked the quilt in around her. The little girl yawned. "Remember we have to go shopping tomorrow to get me a new outfit for the Rock Music Awards."

"I remember."

Serenity burrowed her head into the pillow. "Night, Kiley."

"Night," Kiley said softly, then rose and turned out the light.

11

There had been many times when Esme had sat in the La Verdad coffeehouse in Echo Park with Jorge and his father, Roberto. As she stepped inside, she tried to think back to the very first time she'd met them. It had to be when she'd lived in Fresno. Back then, she'd come to the Echo from time to time with her parents, to visit friends or relatives who lived here. She thought she remembered coming when she was in fifth grade, and meeting Jorge and his father at a Fourth of July picnic in someone's backyard. Yes. That was it. She recalled how she and Jorge had played a funny game of Scrabble together, using both Spanish words and English words. Who had won? She couldn't recall.

This time was totally different. Back then, she hadn't known that Jorge's father was a lawyer, very active in the civil liberties community, as well as being an important figure in Los Angeles Democratic politics. He'd gone to law school at

UCLA, and then, rather than take one of the plum six-figure jobs that were dangled in front of him by law firms galore, he'd opted to go to work for the county public defender's office, representing indigents in criminal cases. Now he was part of a general practice firm of Latino lawyers who did a good deal of public interest law.

She spotted Jorge and his father immediately at a table in the back corner; they waved and she waved back. As usual, La Verdad was crowded, but not the usual neighborhood people coming in for icy homemade *horchata*. Instead, the café had turned into an informal gathering place for people to talk about the Immigration and Customs Enforcement raid. There was a TV turned to Univision on the counter. As Esme made her way back to Roberto and Jorge's table, she took in the grim faces, heard snatches of hushed conversations. So-and-so had been arrested. So-and-so was trying to find a lawyer. So-and-so had papers, but the Feds didn't believe them. Tense. So tense.

Roberto stood. He was an older version of Jorge, dressed in a rumpled gray suit and a white shirt open at the collar. *"Hija mía,"* he said affectionately, hugging Esme and calling her "daughter" in Spanish. "Come sit. There is *horchata* for you already."

Esme slid into the chair next to Jorge. "Thanks, but I'm not thirsty. I'm too worried."

"About your parents," Roberto responded. "I'm worried too."

"My father's been on the phone almost nonstop since I first told him," Jorge relayed.

"Has it done any good?" Esme asked hopefully.

"I'm not sure yet." Roberto rubbed his temples tiredly.

"The ICE is looking to make a name for itself, I think," Jorge said. "That's why they're being so tough on this particular raid. Your parents were just in the wrong place at the wrong time."

This was not good news, this lack of reassurance. She'd hoped Roberto would say that he'd talked to people he knew in the government, and that her parents had nothing to worry about. But now those hopes were dashed.

"Where are your parents now?" Roberto asked.

"In Alhambra with friends. They left the Goldhagens'."

"I talked with Steven Goldhagen earlier. We're working our sources," Roberto confided.

A waitress that Esme knew moved to their table. Her name was Maria but everyone called her Sad Eyes. Esme had gone to her quinceañera when Sad Eyes turned fifteen. Since then, her big brother had been shot in a drive-by, and Sad Eyes had given birth to a little girl and dropped out of school.

"¿Qué pasa, chica?" Sad Eyes asked. "What's up with you, Esme? Still livin' it up in Beverly Hills?"

"Bel Air," Esme automatically corrected. "How's your girl?"

Sad Eyes grinned, and her thin face lit up. "She just turned two and got her ears pierced. She's great." Then her face darkened again. "But my cousin Raphael got caught in that raid."

"My parents, too," Esme told her.

Sad Eyes just shook her head. "You want to order somethin'?"

"No, thanks. Nice to see you," Esme said, and Sad Eyes moved off.

"Raphael was the only boy in that family who didn't

become a gangbanger," Jorge said. "Ironic, huh?" He sipped his coffee.

"It just—it makes me so angry!" Esme exclaimed. "These are good people that got arrested. They have jobs that the gringos don't want."

"And the rich man who owns Consolidated gets cheap labor, doesn't have to pay them any benefits," Jorge added. "He's the one who should be penalized."

An older man named Paco approached the table, hat in hand. He looked immeasurably sad. Esme had no idea what his last name was, but she knew him because of his popular "roach coach"—a street stall that sold homemade tacos and tortillas to the lunch crowd downtown.

"*¿Don Roberto?*" Paco's voice was high-pitched and almost reverent in tone, and he used the form of address meant to convey respect, though Roberto was two or three decades younger than this wrinkled man in dungarees and a clean black shirt.

"*¿Sí, Don Paco?*" Roberto's response was unfailingly polite.

"*Mi hermana, mis hermanos. Todos están con el ICE.*"

Esme drew her breath as Jorge frowned and Roberto nodded thoughtfully. They all listened as Paco shared his story— his sister and two of his brothers from Jalisco had been working under the table for Consolidated and had been arrested in the big raid. They were currently being held in federal custody. Paco handed Roberto a much-folded piece of notebook paper with their names printed on it.

Roberto put the paper in his briefcase, and promised to do what he could to help. Paco went on about how he would come up with a payment plan, but Roberto insisted that Paco was not to worry about the cost. The older man thanked him profusely, and then moved away. It nearly broke Esme's heart.

"What have you done, exactly?" she asked Jorge's father. She knew from experience that feeling sad about a situation didn't help things at all. You had to harden your heart and take action.

For the next five minutes, Roberto listed everything he had done. Not just to protect Esme's parents, who hadn't been arrested, but also for eight or ten residents of the neighborhood who'd been swept up in the immigration raid. He'd negotiated with Immigration and Customs Enforcement, called the mayor's office, called a congressman with whom he was friendly, and gone down to the United States Marshals' office to meet with the detainees. But this was one of those situations where the government was playing it close to the vest.

"Your parents were lucky to get away," Roberto told her.

"They said ICE was taking pictures. They said—"

"Shhhh!" Someone in the front of the café shouted for everyone to be quiet. "*¡Cállate!* The television! About the raid!"

Esme's eyes went to the TV on the counter, as did everyone else's. Univision's *telenovela* was interrupted for a special report on the events at Consolidated. Esme watched in shock as the breathless reporter standing outside the ICE headquarters downtown reported on the scope of the raid. Three hundred and twenty people had been taken into federal custody. The company had been shut down. The detainees were going to be processed quickly and deported. And then, the no-nonsense spokesman for the agency stood by the reporter and issued a chilling warning.

"We know that there were many people at Consolidated who managed to elude our first attempt to enforce the law of the land. But we know who they are, and we will find them. When we do find them, we will prosecute them to the fullest extent of the law, including immediate deportation to their nation of origin. The smartest thing they can do, to avoid any risk of injury in the course of an arrest, is to turn themselves in to law enforcement immediately."

Esme and Jorge locked eyes as Roberto blew out a quick breath, and the café quickly erupted in frenzied conversation.

"They know who they are," Esme repeated dully.

"Your parents said they were filming," Jorge said. "Dad, there must be something else we can do."

Roberto frowned. "I don't know. I think I'd better get back to my office. I have a long night ahead."

Esme thanked him, then Roberto hugged them both and stepped toward the door, stopping to talk for at least a moment with the dozens of people who approached him for reassurance that he really couldn't give.

"Your father is a great man," Esme told Jorge as she watched Roberto with yet another concerned member of the community. She was ashamed for all the times she had thought Jorge's parents were loco for staying in the Echo when they could move out.

Jorge reached for Esme's hand. "I know you don't want to hear this. But you heard what that jackal from Immigration just said. I think they really are going to track your parents down."

"So do I," Esme agreed. She felt like screaming, or throwing up, or hurting someone. But none of that would do any good. There was one thing she *could* do, though; something that not even Jorge or his father could do. She was the only one who could do it.

She took out her cell phone.

"Who you calling?" Jorge asked.

Esme didn't answer. She knew the digits by heart. And she punched them in.

A half hour later, Esme and Jorge walked up the short gravel driveway on Allison Avenue that led to the front door of her ex-boyfriend's bungalow. Parked in the driveway was his pride and joy, a classic yellow Dodge Charger with a 357 Hemi engine that Junior had modified himself. As gasoline prices had soared, Junior was able to drive his pride and joy less and less, which Esme knew broke his heart. Not that Junior would allow that broken heart to show. He was a *veterano,* a former gang member, who had become a paramedic. He still hung out with his homies, most of whom were still bangers. They looked up to Junior, and Junior tried to convince them that there was a life beyond being a member of Los Locos, the crazies. Esme didn't think he tried hard enough. Once you were in, Junior had been fond of telling Esme, there was only one way out. That way—he always laughed here—meant you wouldn't know you were gone, because you'd be gone too. Literally.

Even now, when Junior had become a paramedic and had left the seamier side of gangbanger life behind, this little bungalow was a safe haven for his friends. The rules were strict. No drugs, no weapons, no fighting. Junior had done overtime shift after overtime shift on the ambulance to buy this place.

He didn't want to have to think about paying the mortgage from inside a jail cell.

"You okay?" Jorge asked her. "This can't be easy for you."

"It isn't." Esme fixed her eyes straight ahead. It wasn't easy, coming back here. She and Junior had broken up at the beginning of the summer, when she'd decided to take the nanny job at the Goldhagens'. Junior had opposed it. He'd said that Esme was an Echo girl, and she'd always be an Echo girl. There was no reason for her to try to be someone she wasn't.

Then, when Esme had hooked up with Jonathan Goldhagen, Junior had been pissed. He was sure that Jonathan was using Esme and sure that it would turn out badly for her, to the point where a couple of Los Locos came to the estate and punched out the Goldhagens' son. Esme had gone ballistic over that one, and had pretty much vowed never to talk to Junior again.

Now here she was, with Jorge, about to ask for Junior's help.

The door swung open even before she clacked the rusty knocker. There he stood, wearing baggy jeans and a muscle T-shirt covered by an open black cotton shirt with the sleeves rolled up. On his forearm was the triple lightning bolt that Esme herself had tattooed—the mark that he was a member of Los Locos.

"Esme," he said, making her name into a caress.

Esme went right to the point. "Junior. I gotta talk to you."

"Hey, Junior," Jorge added.

Junior's dark eyes penetrated Esme's soul. She felt her stomach stir as it always did. This guy was raw. Dangerous. So different from Jorge or Jonathan. Primal, in a way.

"Can we come in?" Esme asked.

"*You* can come in. Not this chickenshit," Junior declared. "Jorge, you wait out here. Or go back to the coffeehouse. Or go sit on the curb. I don't fucking care."

Jorge shrugged; he didn't seem to mind. Esme knew that Junior didn't like him, and Jorge knew it, too.

"Fine. I'll meet you back at the coffeehouse," Jorge told Esme.

She agreed, and he left. Junior motioned Esme in.

It was as if she had never left. Same sports on the TV, same Tecate and Dos XXX beer bottles on the table. Same pizza boxes. Same bulletproof glass in the front window.

Junior didn't even ask her to sit down once the front door was closed. He was already up to speed about her parents, because she'd told him on the phone, so he cut right to the chase. "Where are your parents now?"

"With Paco and Maria." Paco and Maria were good friends of theirs who lived in Alhambra. Junior knew them.

"That's smart. They're not at the Goldhagens'."

"Too dangerous, they thought."

Junior nodded. "Nice to see that someone in the family still has some brains."

"Don't be a dick." Esme couldn't help herself. She didn't take shit from anyone, not even Junior.

Junior smiled dangerously. "Careful. You need my help. That's why you're here."

He was right, so she swallowed her pride. "*Mis padres* are scared. I'm scared."

"You gotta know when to hold 'em, know when to fold 'em, baby girl," Junior told her. "Word is, the Feds aren't messing around this time. They'll come after your parents.

Right now, I'd say it's time to fold 'em. You know what we gotta do?"

"I think so, yeah."

Junior ran his fingers through his dark hair. "You gotta get them back to Mexico before ICE catches them and locks them up. I'm gonna do that for you, *esa*. Unofficially."

"Thank you," Esme whispered.

"Can't leave it to you, you don't know what the hell you're doing." He folded his arms, biceps bulging through the thin black cotton of his shirt. "Me and the boys help you out because we remember who you *used* to be."

Esme nodded, accepting the insult. "I appreciate your help more than I can ever say."

"Yeah?" He picked a toothpick up from the table and stuck it in his mouth, letting it dangle from his lower lip. "The big question my boys are going to ask—after how you dissed them—is why should they help you at all?"

12

Chanis—who used only one name—was a personal shopper to the Hollywood elite. Tall, very slender, and Asian American, she had her photo in the gossip rags nearly as often as the stars she dressed. Chanis had finished working with Platinum on her dress for the RMAs, and today the "star" she was dressing was eight-year-old Serenity.

Kiley found this insane. She hadn't even known that famous designers made dresses for the prepubescent set. Well, it turned out that some did. It also turned out that there were designers who made clothes only for this market. Chanis had brought a selection of outfits by both types for Serenity to consider. It would be entirely the girl's choice, too—her mother was missing in action.

Serenity sat cross-legged on her bed as Chanis and a flunky guided a clothing rack into her white-on-white bedroom, which followed the same noncolor scheme as the rest of

Platinum's estate. As they entered, Serenity was casually painting her nails midnight blue, as if having adults bring designer clothes to her room on a rolling rack was an everyday thing.

"Why don't you put the nail polish away now?" Kiley suggested.

Serenity added a blob of blue to the nail on her pinky finger. "When I'm done." Her eyes flicked to Chanis and the flunky, a more diminutive carbon copy of the personal shopper who didn't offer her name. Neither did her boss. Kiley found that very rude. "Which gown did my mom choose?"

"None of them," Chanis replied, shaking her waterfall of inky hair off her face. "Christian Siriano designed something for her and she's going to wear that."

"The guy who won *Project Runway*? I *love* him!" Serenity squealed. "He's fierce. I want him to design something for me, too."

"It's already Tuesday and the awards are Saturday night," Chanis pointed out, unzipping a garment bag. "Not enough time to go from scratch. Next year, assuming your mom is nominated."

"She will be," Serenity declared.

Chanis nodded, probably in the hope that she'd be invited back next year, too. "Okay, you ready to try stuff on?"

"Who'd you bring?" Serenity asked diffidently.

"Flowers by Zoe, Lipstik Girls, cach*cach*," Chanis rattled off. Serenity sighed. "Whatever."

She capped the nail polish bottle and slid off the bed, then pulled her white tank top over her head. She wore a lacy silk training bra, though there was absolutely nothing to train. Meanwhile, Kiley screwed the top on the nail polish. "I need

113

to go check Sid's homework," she told her charge. "Are you good in here for a while without me?"

"Sure. I'm with Chanis. It's not like *you* have taste."

Kiley bit back everything she wanted to say, things like: *stop being so rude; remember that you're only eight; how about working on those manners?* But she didn't say a word. She tried to pick her moments with all three of Platinum's kids. She knew any kind of chastisement in front of Chanis would embarrass Serenity, and that there was nothing worse than public humiliation.

When they were in private, though, she'd have a lot to say. What she couldn't say was "I'll tell your father." She didn't know who Serenity's father was, and Platinum's three children each reportedly had a different dad. Not that any of them ever showed up.

"Okay, I'll check back with you in a little while," Kiley said. She nodded at Chanis. "Just send Serenity if you need me."

She went down the hall to Sid's room—Sid was short for Siddhartha. Like Serenity's room and the entire house, it was all white. Sid, who was now in fifth grade, was sitting at his desk in front of his iBook, with papers and notebooks spilling out of the backpack he'd thrown onto the tufted quilt on his bed. He was wearing jeans and an old Bruce Springsteen concert T-shirt. That was ironic, considering that Springsteen had once—despite any shred of evidence—been rumored to be the father of Platinum's older son, Bruce.

Kiley glanced at the computer screen. Sid was Instant Messaging a friend. He'd recently buzzed off his pale blond hair, much to his mother's displeasure. Around the house, he tended to wear music-oriented baseball-style caps. Here in his room, his skull gleamed.

"Hey, Sid," Kiley greeted him. "Finish up with your friend and get to your homework. Need any help?"

"I'm already doing my homework," Sid said. He kept clicking away at the keyboard.

Kiley sat on his bed and began to put his school stuff into his backpack. "Doesn't look like it."

"I'm working with my friends."

"Oh, you got some kind of group project?" Kiley wondered.

"We got questions on this novel we're reading in class. It's called *Zink*. It's about a girl who has cancer and zebras who can talk. It's really stupid."

Kiley saw the book on the bed and picked it up. The cover was beautiful: a girl gazing into the distance, with zebras and the African plains spreading out behind her. "What page are you on?"

Sid shrugged.

"Come on. You must know how much of it you've read," Kiley persisted.

"I read the first chapter, but that's kinda all I had to read. Reading the whole book, that's not how we do it."

"What do you mean, that's not how we do it? Traditionally, when you're assigned a book for school, the idea is to actually read it."

Sid laughed. "That's so last century. My friends and I, we have a homework ring. Didn't you?"

"No. And maybe you could fill me in, because I've never heard of one." Kiley folded her arms. She knew this was going to be rich.

What followed was Sid's explanation as to what a homework ring was, and how it worked. Essentially, it was a way to cheat. If there were five questions, Sid and four of his friends were each responsible for answering one question. Then they all e-mailed each other their answers, but changed them enough on their own answer sheets so that the teacher couldn't tell they'd copied off each other. They were all careful to make different small mistakes on different questions, so their teacher never got suspicious.

Kiley was appalled.

"You think it's cheating? No it isn't," he insisted.

"Yes it is; you're copying each other's work."

Sid finally turned away from the screen. "So? We save a lot of time."

So? Had the kid really just said *So?*

"You're supposed to do your own work, at home. That's why they call it homework."

Sid shot her a baleful look. "Only losers do that."

For the briefest moment, Kiley wished that the Colonel was still around. Platinum's sister and brother-in-law had moved in when Platinum had been in pretrial detention. The brother-in-law had been a colonel in the United States Marine Corps, and treated the kids as if they were fresh recruits in boot camp. To call it culture shock was an understatement. Kiley could only imagine what the Colonel would say about a homework ring. He'd probably sentence the kids to a month in the stockade.

Just possibly, though, Platinum wouldn't approve of it, either. It was worth a shot.

"I'd really like you to get off the computer and read the novel," Kiley said. "If you don't, I'm going to have to tell your mother."

"Ha! I already told her. She said she wished she'd thought of that when she was in school. Hey, Daphne just sent me the answer to question three."

Sid opened up the e-mail as Kiley realized that he was probably telling the truth about having told his own mother about the homework ring. Platinum was hardly an advocate of book learning. To her, school was nothing more than society's way of trying to stifle kids' creativity.

Kiley gave up. "I'll be in Serenity's room if you need me."

"Cool." Sid was already cutting and pasting Daphne's answer into his own answer sheet. "I won't. If you get bored with my sister come on back. I'll show you how it works so you can do it for me next time."

Then he looked at her. "Wanna read the book and write me some coverage?"

"This place makes the best milk shakes," Kiley said, briefly taking her mouth away from the straw.

It was two hours later. She and Matt had met for what was supposed to be coffee at Johnny Rockets on Melrose, but she'd opted for a milk shake instead. Vanilla, so thick you could eat it with a spoon if you wanted to, and so large that after you drained the huge sundae glass, you could pour more in from the metal shaker.

"I'm jealous," Matt said, sipping his black coffee. He patted his abs. "I've got a photo shoot tomorrow. Every pound shows."

Kiley wiped her lips. "The downside of modeling, huh?"

"Yeah." Matt grinned. "But I'd be an asshole to complain about it. And let's face it, L.A. has enough assholes."

Kiley laughed. She liked Matt. Today he wore jeans and a

sky blue T-shirt under an Italian cotton sport jacket, managing to look casually elegant and almost absurdly hip at the same time. But it wasn't just that he was easy on the eyes, almost as easy on the eyes as Tom. He was cheerful, low-key, funny, and he hadn't hit on her. She was glad for that. She was also glad that he'd mentioned some girl he was crushing on. That made it safe. Mostly.

If Kiley was going to be completely honest, Tom had a lot to do with the new friendship. They often ended up talking about him. And since Matt had known Tom long before Kiley had, she got all kinds of great information about him. Who helped him in his career when he came to Los Angeles, the companies he had modeled for—that kind of thing. Tom was way too modest to talk about himself like that, and Kiley wasn't the kind of girl who Googled and ZabaSearched just out of curiosity.

Talking with Matt was much more satisfying than moaning about how much she missed him to Esme or Lydia. Esme had much bigger problems right now with her parents, and Lydia was consumed with her new friendship with Audrey Birnbaum.

"Heard from Tom?" Matt asked, almost as if Kiley had willed him to do so.

"I did," she replied happily. "We texted earlier today. They're still in Moscow but they start shooting in Tver tomorrow. He said he's fallen in love with Russian food."

"Better than with Russian women," Matt joked.

Kiley nodded. "They are *so* beautiful. Those cheekbones."

"Oh hey, speaking of cheekbones, Marym sent me some great photos. I think Tom is in a couple."

Marym. Not Kiley's favorite person. And the feeling was

pretty much mutual. Yes, Kiley had been part of a demonstration outside of Marym's Malibu home to protest against privatizing the beach. And yes, Kiley had assumed that Marym was a shallow snob and had treated her badly. But the Israeli supermodel hadn't been a princess to her, either.

"She and I didn't exactly hit it off," Kiley said. She knew if she had any guts, she would have admitted she was jealous as hell. Oh well.

"She can seem aloof if you don't know her," Matt explained. "But she's a total sweetheart, really."

"I'll take your word for it." She drank again from her milk shake.

Matt eyed Kiley over his coffee cup. "You do know she and Tom are just buds."

"So he tells me."

"It's true," Matt insisted. He hesitated. "Man, I was going to show you the photos, but—"

Something inside Kiley went on red alert. "But what?"

"You know Marym's been asked to be in the movie?"

Kiley nearly choked. "Since when?"

"You gotta read the trades. Here. Wait."

Matt spotted a copy of the new issue of *Variety* on the empty table next to theirs. One quick motion and he nabbed it. One more motion and he flipped to a small story in the middle of the issue about Tom's movie. "Look."

There it was. In black and white. Marym had just been added to the cast, playing a Russian Jewish woman who was torn between staying in Moscow to help with the honky-tonk or emigrating to Israel.

Great. Imagine which she'd pick.

Kiley put the puzzle pieces together. "I guess she and Tom are hanging out. She sent you some pictures?"

Matt shook his head. "Look, forget I even mentioned it—"

"I'm fine," Kiley forced herself to say. "I'd really like to see them."

"I never should've brought it up," Matt mumbled.

Kiley held out her hand, palm up. *Give me the photos.*

He reached into his jacket pocket, took out some photos he'd printed off his e-mail, and handed them over to Kiley. The quality wasn't so great—they were on regular paper and not photo paper, and the printer wasn't the best—but Kiley saw all she needed to see and more.

Marym with a bunch of Russian models, blowing kisses to the camera in Red Square.

Marym with two other models in a nightclub.

Marym outside a casino.

Marym and another girl eating something unidentifiable in Gorky Park.

Marym kissing Tom.

Kiley nearly dropped the photo, as if it had burned her hand. Then she tightened her grip and studied the shot. It was a close-up, impossible to tell where they were. Marym's eyes were closed, her lips on Tom's. Correction—his were on hers. The guy she loved was definitely kissing Marym back.

13

Flipper was murmuring into Lydia's ear. "I grew up in Hollywood. My dad is an agent at CAA. He reps some of the biggest people in the business," he confided. "But I gotta tell you—this is freakin' unbelievable."

Lydia leaned into his muscular shoulder and looked around Nate 'n' Al's, a landmark Beverly Hills deli. "If you're lyin', you're dyin'," she agreed.

It was the next day, at lunchtime, just before the late-afternoon RMA rehearsal at the Kodak Theatre. The high school was out of session because of a teacher in-service day, so Lydia didn't even have to skip school to go to rehearsal. After Kiley got Serenity, Sid, and Bruce off to school, she was free, too. Esme had called and told them she'd meet them there later, that things with her parents were really bad; they might even have to return to Mexico. The whole thing, she said, would be resolved today. There was still a chance that either Steven or Jorge's father could defuse the crisis, but Esme had to spend the day preparing for any and all eventualities.

When Lydia had left her aunt's estate, Audrey was still fast asleep—Lydia knew Audrey didn't have to rehearse until later that afternoon, so she didn't wake her. When Lydia had shown up at the Kodak, Kiley was already there. They spent two hours stuffing inserts into three thousand programs, putting name cards on fifteen hundred seats in the bottom tiers in accordance with a seating chart Jocelyn handed them when they arrived, and personally e-mailing about a hundred seat-fillers, whose job was to fill the seats for any down-front attendees who needed to take a bathroom break. "Empty seats on TV are death," Jocelyn told them. "If there are any, I'm holding you personally responsible."

The work was tedious. That a trained monkey could do it was obvious to Lydia. However, the trained monkey would not appreciate the sound track—some of the best singers and bands in the world were onstage rehearsing while Lydia and Kiley went about their mundane tasks: Coldplay, Fergie, Usher, Justin Timberlake.

Audrey wandered in around one; she and Platinum weren't scheduled to rehearse until four o'clock. When the stage manager called a lunch break, Audrey told Lydia that she was going to lunch with some of her mates, and would Lydia like to join them? There was a famous delicatessen in Beverly Hills called Nate 'n' Al's,' right on Rodeo Drive. That was where they'd be, and if Lydia wanted to call a friend to meet them, that was fine too.

Lydia's first thought was to ask Kiley, but her friend had been commandeered to make another one of those food runs to the Grove for show personnel who wouldn't be leaving the theater. So Lydia had called Flipper, who was out surfing by Will Rogers Beach. Would he like to join Lydia, Audrey, and a bunch of rock stars for lunch? She didn't have to ask him twice. He said he'd meet her there in twenty minutes; he just had to load up his van with his surfboard and get out of his wet suit.

Flipper arrived in time for the main course. By then, Audrey and Lydia were at a table for ten. There was one older man who Lydia thought was Clive Davis, top record producer of all time—she'd seen him on *American Idol*. She also recognized John Mayer with some blonde, Adam Levine from Maroon 5, and Fergie, who was dressed down in pink sweats, a baseball cap, and huge sunglasses.

Flipper wore jeans and a black long-sleeved T-shirt. He slid into the seat Lydia had saved to her right. It turned out that he actually knew Mr. Davis because of his dad, and they chatted like old friends.

Evidently Clive Davis's assistant had ordered for the table before they arrived, and the food kept coming and coming—huge platters of fresh-baked bagels and trays of pastrami, corned beef, and even pickled tongue. Back in Amazonia, every part of a hunted animal was consumed by the tribesmen, so when most of the people at the table turned up their noses at the tongue, Lydia chowed down happily. There were also potato knishes, cheese and blueberry blintzes, a tureen of chicken noodle soup with matzoh balls, kasha, pickled green tomatoes and cucumbers, and a dessert called halvah that was made from ground sesame seeds. Lydia thought it was the best thing she'd ever tasted.

The most fun of all, though, was the attention she and the rest of the table were getting from other diners. Nate 'n' Al's attracted a very mixed crowd: agents from William Morris, whose offices were just down the street, tourists checking out the stores on Rodeo Drive, musicians, performers, directors, and just ordinary ladies who lunched. All of them except for the tourists were used to seeing celebrities in bars and restaurants. It was normally no more noteworthy than spotting a squirrel. Lydia realized, however, that this table was an exception. It was so star-studded that patrons kept figuring out reasons to pass by on a roundabout trip to the deli counter or the bathroom. Many of them snapped photographs with their cell phones. Lydia liked that. A lot. It made her feel as if she was where she belonged.

"Any word on what you'll be doing during the awards Saturday night?" Flipper asked as he bit into a sesame bagel slathered with cream cheese.

"Not a clue," Lydia said. "If it's something glamorous I'm shit out of luck. I don't have a gown to wear."

"I thought you stole stuff from your aunt," Audrey said.

"I borrow," Lydia corrected, "I don't steal. And my aunt doesn't do gowns. When she has to get dressed up she goes for a tuxedo."

Flipper grinned. "You'd look cute in a tuxedo."

Lydia shook her head. The girl with John Mayer snuggled under his heavily tattooed arm and moved in for a very public display of affection. *Desperate for attention,* Lydia thought. *Of course, I wouldn't mind kissing him myself. . . .*

"So, you gonna go for the tux, sweets?" Audrey asked Lydia.

"Not really my style. And I don't have money for a dress."

"You shouldn't let money stop you," the rock star told her, lighting a cigarette until Clive told her that even though she was who she was, they were not going to let her smoke in any restaurant in Los Angeles.

"Bloody uptight Americans," she groused, stubbing the cigarette out on the edge of her plate. She put her hands on her stomach. "I ate my bloody weight just now. Balls."

This struck Lydia as hilarious. Audrey was teeny-tiny, with a stomach that was practically concave.

"I need some bloody exercise after that feed," Audrey said. She slid out of her chair. "Lydia?"

"You want me to come with you?" Lydia asked.

"Your friend Phil won't mind," Audrey said. "Right, Phil?"

"Flipper," he corrected easily. "Not a problem. I'm fine."

"I agree," said a flirtatious girl whose name Lydia had never caught. She had great red hair, huge green eyes, even huger fake boobs popping out of her low-cut T-shirt, and a serious case of lips overstuffed with collagen, also known as trout pout.

Flipper smiled at her. "Thanks."

Flipper was *such* a flirt. Which bothered Lydia not at all. She gave him a quick kiss goodbye and took off with Audrey.

"Where are we going?" Lydia asked as they hit the bright daylight and the blast of hot air on the street.

"Mystery trip, ducks," Audrey replied.

Fair enough. A mystery trip with one of the biggest rock stars in the world, whom she could now call her friend and who was living at her place for a week. What could be bad? Nothing. What could be good? All she had to do was go along and find out.

They never even had to get into a car to reach their destination. The Valentino boutique was at 360 Rodeo Drive, an easy walk from the restaurant. It had a white storefront with two huge picture windows, and the name of the store etched into the stone above in big block letters. Audrey had called ahead as they walked. Not only did a personal saleswoman meet them at the door, but the boutique was also closed for an hour so that Audrey could shop without getting harassed.

The saleswoman introduced herself as Lily. She had a deep Lauren Bacall kind of voice, curly red hair, and porcelain skin. She wore a perfect black pencil skirt and a pale lavender silk blouse with a dozen strands of pearls gracing her swanlike neck. If she was impressed by being with the great Audrey Birnbaum, she didn't let it show.

"Hello, Ms. Birnbaum," Lily said. "Nice to meet you."

"Call me Audrey or I'll look around for me old lady," Audrey groused. "This is my friend Lydia."

"Hey," Lydia said. She was not easily intimidated.

"Treat her like she's my family, Lily," Audrey ordered.

"My pleasure," Lily said smoothly. "What are you looking for, Lydia?"

"I'm not," Lydia said, because now she was quite confused. She was happy to accompany Audrey on a shopping trip; it was exciting to see that Audrey had the kind of clout where they'd close the shop for her, but Lydia was definitely not looking to shop for herself. She reckoned there was nothing in this boutique with a price tag that didn't go at least four digits.

"I'm buying you a gown," Audrey explained. Before Lydia could protest, Audrey launched into an explanation for Lily: Lydia would be attending the Rock Music Awards and she needed a killer gown. Money was irrelevant; the only criterion was that it should make Lydia look hotter than she'd ever looked in her life.

Lydia liked that idea. But she could also hear her mother's voice in her head, saying she should refuse such an extravagant gift.

She mentally told her mother to hush and just said, "Thank you."

Lily gave Lydia the once-over. "A size four, but busty," she concluded. "Some of the designers don't make clothes for women with curves," she confided. "So, let's get started. Color?"

"White, maybe?" Audrey suggested to Lydia. "Or silver?"

"Or red?" Lydia asked hopefully. "Or magenta?"

"Got it. I'll be right back. I've got just the thing."

Lily didn't go to one of the clothing racks. Instead, she headed into a back room, while Audrey and Lydia were ushered by an assistant to a couple of comfortable padded chairs, and offered flutes of champagne.

"Is this how you always shop?" Lydia asked, enjoying the sensation of the champagne bubbles tickling her tongue.

"Either this or else I order online and skip the whole ordeal," Audrey said. "Fame has its drawbacks."

Lily returned with four gowns over her arm. "Shall we go back to the dressing room so that you can try them on?"

"Shall we see what we're dealing with first?" Audrey suggested.

Lily had an assistant hold up the gowns one by one. The first was a bias-cut silver silk with sequins around the navel and a low neckline. The second was lipstick red, a strapless chiffon. The third was white, with pin tucks and a draped back. And the fourth was a rich magenta silk, cinched under the bust and flowing to the floor with a slit up one leg.

"That one," Lydia said, pointing to the magenta gown. "It's perfect."

"Well then, go try it on, ducks," Audrey urged. "I'll wait here and enjoy the bubbly."

Lily led the way to the dressing room, which was as big as the guest cottage Lydia lived in. The walls were pink-and-white-striped wallpaper, the carpeting a thick cream color. Lydia was not at all shy about nudity. She whipped off her clothes while Lily stood there and helped her into the dress.

"You can't wear a bra with it," Lily said. "But there's boning under the bust; you won't need one."

Lydia took off her sheer black Chantilly bra and Lily dropped the dress over her head. The silk fell around her feet. Lydia lifted her girls above the boning, and when Lily zipped the gown, she had cleavage for days.

"Oh my," Lily breathed.

"Dang, I could go gay for me," Lydia joked to her own reflection. Lily didn't laugh. "Joking," she explained.

Lily smiled on cue. It occurred to Lydia that when you were famous, people never really acted normal around you.

Lydia glanced down at the tiny price tag held to the dress with a minute gold pin. She couldn't help herself. She peeked. The dress was more than five thousand dollars.

"Of course, you still need shoes," Lily said.

"Got 'em." The door opened and Audrey walked in with a pair of deep purple satin pumps dangling from her fingers. "They were in the window," she told Lydia. "Holy shit, you look bloody fantastic in that."

"I'm sorry, Ms. Birnbaum, but those shoes are only for display—" Lily began.

"If they fit my friend here, they're no longer for display. You an eight?"

Lydia nodded. She stepped into the sky-high pumps. The open toe was surrounded by crystals.

"That's the dress and those are the shoes," Audrey pronounced. "Weren't you easy to shop for."

"I don't know how to begin to thank you," Lydia said as Lily carefully unzipped her.

"We're friends, ducks," Audrey said simply. "Share and share alike, I always say." She plucked a credit card from her purse and handed it to Lily, then Lydia pulled on her jeans, bra, and T-shirt.

"Is there a reason you're being this nice to me?" Lydia asked. Maybe this was all a lead-up to hitting on her. But no, Audrey had talked about the mad affair she was having with her bass player, a tall, thin Jamaican guy.

"Not hitting on you, ducks." Audrey slung an arm around Lydia's shoulder. "Here's how I see it. Guys come and go, but girlfriends are forever."

Dang. One of the most famous rock singers in the world

just *liked* her, and was doing nice things for her because of that. Lydia thought that if she was in the same position, she'd do the same for Esme and Kiley. Still, it was awfully fun to be the recipient of this kind of largesse.

"Then I'll say thank you," Lydia told her, giving her friend a hug. "Because for real? This is the greatest day of my life."

"And it'll just keep getting better," Audrey promised. "Got to get to the Kodak for rehearsal. But later tonight? Par-tay!"

14

Esme stood by the front-gate intercom; she'd been pacing back and forth for the past thirty minutes waiting for the buzzer to sound. Still, when it did, indicating that Junior was down at the gate with her parents, she jumped anyway.

She pushed the Talk button. "Yeah."

"'S me, Esme." Junior's voice was direct. "I got your parents."

"I'll buzz you in and meet you in front."

Esme pushed the silver button that would open the front gate, and turned on the closed-circuit security camera that allowed her to see—in living color—as the huge metal gate opened and Junior drove through.

She remembered the first time she'd come to this property with Junior, to pick her parents up from work, never dreaming that she'd ever work there herself. The intercom had been broken, and the Bel Air police had shown up to question the two brown young people in the piece-of-crap car outside the fancy gates.

She sighed, so weary. Last night had been one of the longest of her life. She'd spent it sprawled on her bed, staring up at the same exposed beams that stars like Clark Gable had seen when, according to legend, they'd stayed in this very guesthouse. Her parents were such a big part of her life. They were the reason that she was even here at the Goldhagens' place. She loved them with all her heart. Her mother had better judgment than anyone she'd ever met. The idea that today would be the last time she'd see them on American soil for who knew how long was almost impossible to contemplate. No more going "home" to the Echo to see them. No more finding her mother cooking tortillas in the cramped kitchen, her face lined with exhaustion after a long day working at the Goldhagens'. No more hugs. No more having her father stroke her hair and kiss her forehead, and show her how to fix a carburetor with nothing more than ingenuity and stuff lying around the house, or replaster a wall, or grow a perfect orchid.

No more. They were going back to Mexico.

Not that their getting in was a sure thing. In recent months, the border patrol had stepped up their enforcement efforts. There was no reason to be sure that crossing southbound in the desert would be any easier than crossing northbound. Plus, there were new sections of security fence designed to block human traffic from Mexico into the USA, but which were equally efficient against wrong-way passage. Junior had supposedly found a so-called coyote, a Mexican guy who specialized in illegal border crossings, to get her

132

parents across. Now he was bringing her folks here for this hard goodbye. Diane and Steven, along with the twins, were already at the gazebo by the tennis court, where the cook and one of the maids had set out a buffet breakfast.

On the closed-circuit, Esme saw the Charger pull into the driveway. She took a deep breath. She would not cry in front of her *madre* and *padre,* no matter what. Would not, would not, would not. It would make them feel terrible, as if they had to comfort her. No way was she putting them through that on top of everything else.

She went outside, where her parents were already getting out of Junior's car. One look into her mother's eyes was all she needed to see that her mom was scared. Very scared. As for her father, his face was frozen in a stoic mask.

"Go around the back, to the gazebo," she told them in Spanish.

"Steven and Diane are there?" Her mother's voice was somber.

"And the twins. I want to talk to Junior. I'll be there in a minute."

Esme went around to the driver's side, where Junior still sat. She tapped on the window; he rolled it down. He wore a short-sleeved black cotton shirt and black trousers.

"I wanted to thank you," she said simply.

"You're welcome." Junior's eyes were hidden behind dark sunglasses. Still, he faced the windshield rather than facing her. "A half hour, no more. Louie's waiting."

"Louie?"

"He'll take them to Calexico. Then he'll hand them over to someone else who'll get them across."

133

Esme couldn't help herself—she had to ask. "What's this going to cost?"

"I ever mention money to you?" Junior asked sharply.

"No," Esme admitted.

Finally he turned to her, his eyes still hidden behind the glasses. "Just remember who you are and where you come from. You got that?"

She nodded.

"And remember who you turned to when the shit went down. That's all I ask." Junior tapped his watch. "Half an hour. Clock's ticking."

To emphasize his point, Junior put in a set of earbuds to his MP3 player, and leaned back against the black headrest. She was dismissed.

Esme made her way along the gravel path that led to the brown oak gazebo near the tennis court. Diane, Steven, the twins, and her parents sat around an oval table. The twins were chattering away, oblivious to the glum adults. When the girls saw Esme, they immediately tore away from the table and ran up the path so that they could each grab one of her hands and walk her to the outdoor breakfast. They were dressed identically, in pink shorts, long-sleeved pink tops, and white Reebok running shoes. Esme knew that their outfits, which looked simple enough, were in fact from the Pampered Princess boutique on Rodeo Drive, and the tops alone had run more than a hundred dollars.

"We don't have school this morning," Weston singsonged.

"We're having a picnic instead," Easton chimed in, clearly impressed by this change in the usual school-morning routine.

134

Esme was impressed with how great their English was getting. "That's pretty exciting."

"Why don't we have school?" Weston asked.

"Well, it's a little party," Esme explained. "A special one." This seemed to satisfy them for the moment. She slid into the empty chair next to her mother.

"Good morning, Esme," Diane said.

"Morning."

Steven gave her a sympathetic look over his glass of fresh-squeezed orange juice. "Try to eat something," he coaxed.

On any other day, the food would have been appetizing. Stacks of bagels fresh from the oven, plates filled with fresh-cut lox, three different kinds of cream cheese, homemade croissants and sweet rolls, sliced apples for the girls—one of the few healthy treats they loved—and pitchers of fresh-squeezed juice. Only the twins were eating, munching away on the apple slices. The adults just stared into their coffees.

Diane kindly filled a ceramic cup for Esme, adding sugar and milk, and handed it to her.

"Thanks." Esme took a sip just to be polite.

"Should you tell the twins, or should Diane and I?" Steven asked.

"English or Spanish?" Diane added. Though she was impeccably turned out as always—fresh manicure, perfectly streaked blond hair tumbling around her shoulders—her eyes looked tense, with quote marks of concern between her brows.

If she knew about those marks, she'd already be at the spa getting them injected with Botox, Esme thought, apropos of nothing at all except her reluctance to deal with the sad matter at hand. Cleo, Diane's toy poodle, who today had a pink and white polka-dotted bow with matching pink and white polished nails, sat in the shade of the table, her head on Diane's sandaled foot. Diane reached down and fed Cleo some morsels.

Esme momentarily wished she was the dog. No worries for Cleo.

So, who should tell the twins that once again, people they cared about who spoke their native tongue were leaving their life? Esme felt guilty enough about her own part in this, having left the girls so easily, not really considering what the effect would be on them. That was one of the many reasons she wanted to be the one to tell the twins about her parents: to make up for that, to reassure the girls that she wouldn't leave again.

But it wasn't really her responsibility. In the long run, the more the girls bonded with Steven and Diane as their parents, the better off they'd be.

"You tell them. If they have questions in Spanish, I'll answer them."

"Sounds good," Steven acknowledged.

Diane's gaze flicked to her daughters just as Easton handed Estella an apple slice and smiled.

"Just get it over with," Esme told him.

Steven did. He got the girls' attention, then slowly and patiently, with some help from Diane, told them that Señor and Señora Castaneda were going to be returning home to Mexico today, but that Esme would be staying. The twins asked if Señor and Señora would come back like Esme had. Steven said he wasn't sure. Then they asked if the Castanedas had family in Mexico. Steven said they did.

In "Ciudad Juárez," Estella told the girls in Spanish, stroking Easton's hair. "But we're going to Jalisco. To a beautiful city on the ocean called Puerto Vallarta."

"Why are you leaving?" Weston asked, wide-eyed. "Did you get a better job?"

Steven seemed to hesitate, so Esme spoke up. "My parents are Mexican. So they're going home."

Easton looked as if she was going to cry. She whispered in her twin's ear. "Sister says we're from Colombia," Weston explained. "Does that mean we have to go back?"

Diane rose and hugged both little girls. "This is your home now and we're your family—Daddy and me and Jonathan—forever and ever."

Weston scrunched up her face, trying to understand. "But Esme is their family forever."

Steven looked helplessly at Diane. One of the most powerful men in Hollywood obviously didn't know what to say. He clearly didn't want to get into the legalities of immigration with his children, who had so many abandonment issues of their own. Yes, they were doing reasonably well in America, but that didn't mean their anxiety level couldn't go over the top.

"How about if we take the twins back to the house and talk to them," Diane proposed.

Steven agreed, and Esme liked the idea of a few minutes alone with her mother and father. So with the request that the Castanedas stop and say goodbye before they left, Steven and

Diane took the girls back to the main mansion. Esme was alone with her parents. Finally.

They spoke in Spanish. It was so much easier, Esme thought as they talked, so much more nuanced and expressive. Spanish was an emotional language, and this was an emotional time.

"Don't worry," she reassured them, even though she didn't really feel confident at all. "Junior will take care of you. Just do what his men say and you'll be fine." She took an envelope out of her purse and handed it to her mother. In it was a thousand dollars. She promised to send more money to them regularly.

Her mother refused to take it.

"Junior said to take no money," her father explained. "We'll probably get shaken down in the desert. We'll have just a little, Esme." Her father rubbed his temples wearily. "Ah. How did it come to this?"

"I'll wire you this money," Esme promised.

Her father shook his head. "Keep it for yourself. Mr. Goldhagen is helping us get jobs at the resort; we'll be fine."

Esme didn't bother arguing. She was still going to send them money. "You'll stay with Uncle Agosto?"

Her father nodded. "He moved to Puerto Vallarta. We'll call you as soon as we cross the border."

Esme blew some air between her lips. This was all so direct. So matter-of-fact. Not really of the heart.

"Steven told me about your jobs at the resort," Esme began. "And he said he would pay for me to come visit you. . . ."

"He is a very wonderful man," her mother said.

In some ways, yes, Esme agreed. But in others? Making her

138

parents wear uniforms to work for no good reason at all? That was so demeaning. Not offering them health insurance, or benefits of any kind? That was not so wonderful. Esme doubted that it had ever even occurred to Steven and Diane.

Now her father spoke. "What we want for you, daughter, is to live honestly, with pride. Do nothing to make us ashamed."

"We want you to finish school, Esme," her mother said. "That's why you came to Bel Air and got out of the Echo, not to make money putting tattoos on people's skin. We don't care what makes the most money. We care what kind of person you will be. We want you to be an educated person."

Her father nodded gravely. "Go back to high school. Then go to college. That is what we have always wanted for you. Why we do everything that we do. For you."

Esme sighed. Even now, at this terrible moment, her hackles rose at being told what to do. What was *wrong* with her?

"I'll consider all that," Esme promised. Then she felt tears in the back of her throat. She willed them away, gulping hard. "I'll . . . I'm going to miss you. So much."

She flung herself into her mother's arms, and then stretched an arm out and beckoned for her father to join the hug. He did, and they clung to each other for nearly a minute, until Esme whispered that they'd better go, that Junior was waiting for them. She walked them as far as her guesthouse, then kissed them both, hugged them again, and watched them walk up the path. Going with them all the way to Junior's car would be too hard. She would wave goodbye from here.

Once they were out of sight, though, she couldn't help herself. The tears came. She dragged herself to the guesthouse and sat in one of the white rocking chairs that the Goldhagens had recently put on the porch, burying her hands in her face.

"It's hard, huh?"

She looked up. There was Jonathan Goldhagen, wearing a tennis shirt and jeans, his face open and sympathetic.

"Someone looks like she needs a hug," he said softly.

It was tempting. She could already picture herself rushing into his embrace. But there was no safety there, she reminded herself. And there never would be. She would never feel as though she really belonged in his world. She would always be a visitor, always feel less than, whether it was true or not; needy, insecure, a version of herself she didn't even like.

"Someone needs to be left alone," she forced herself to say.

She eyed him, willing him to leave. Finally, he did. As his feet crunched in the gravel, she buried her face in her hands again, and cried until she didn't think she could muster another tear. She fooled herself when she discovered there were plenty more, saved up for so long, and for so many reasons.

When she finally stopped crying, she felt alone, abandoned. She got up and went into the guesthouse, the screen door banging behind her like a firing squad at her own execution.

15

"It's Lyrik with a *k*," the curvaceous brunette told Kiley and
Lydia, shaking her long chestnut hair off her shoulders with
what was obviously a practiced gesture. "I'm Jocelyn's assistant. When I'm talking, pretend it's her talking."

Lyrik with a *k* had eye-popping breasts and wore a tight
pink T-shirt with what Kiley assumed were the designer jeans
of the moment.

Not that Kiley had any clue what designer that might be.
She'd been around Hollywood long enough to know the
drill. One day you were the designer everyone just had to
wear. The next day you were consigned to the sale rack, or
to one of the many high-end preowned clothing shops that
sprang up around the city. From there, it was just one more
step down to Goodwill.

Kiley and Lydia were one floor up from the actual Kodak
Theatre, in a cavernous room that right now contained nothing

but a pile of large boxes stacked against one wall and stacks of folding tables. There was also a pile of red and black Rock Music Awards tablecloths on the floor, and a huge stack of oversized canvas bags with the signature red and black Rock Music Awards logo.

It was Thursday, late afternoon; the awards show was just forty-eight hours away. Lydia had actually gone to school that day—she seemed to miss more than she attended—and afterward Kiley had driven them here and parked in the underground lot at the Renaissance Hotel, adjacent to the theater.

Esme had called and told them where to be and when to be there. Kiley had pressed for more information about what was going on with Esme's parents, but Esme had been terse. All she said was that she'd meet them at the Kodak and she'd get there when she got there.

As for where they were, they were in the swag room of the awards. Or, as Lyrik put it, "At least it will be after you guys get done with it."

"The high-end freebies," Lydia translated, with relish for said freebies apparent in her tone.

"For the VIPs. That lets you two out. Damn. How did this happen?" Lyrik glared at a chipped nail on her left hand.

"I'd just like to point out that insulting the volunteers is not real productive," Lydia drawled sweetly.

Kiley stifled a laugh, but Lyrik stayed all business.

"I wouldn't be joking when you two figure out how much work there is. Your job is to set up the tables, set up the clothing racks when they get here, cover the tables in tablecloths, and unload all those boxes. This chart should help you. Don't mess it up or you'll have to start at the beginning. I'm serious."

Lyrik thrust a sheet of paper at Kiley, then looped some of her lustrous hair behind one ear and peered around. "I was told there were three people working in here. Where's the third?"

"Our friend Esme isn't here yet," Kiley explained.

"Fun, fun, more fun for you." Lyrik smiled at them, showing white teeth too glistening to not have had the help of a laser.

"What if we get hungry?" Lydia asked.

"Craft Service downstairs is for VIPs only," Lyrik reminded them. "There's a table set up outside with some stuff for you guys. Or maybe there's vending machines. I'll check back." She pivoted on her four-inch sunshine yellow open-toe pump and left.

"Vending machines? We get to use the vending machines? Did you see the spread for the VIPs? We got to eat at Craft Service yesterday." Lydia was very unhappy.

Kiley knew it wouldn't help their cause to mope. She looked at the instructions Lyrik had given her. "Okay. We start by setting up the tables in this order. And the tablecloths. Then we go to boxes marked one through five, and put one of everything that's inside them into the Jewels and Pinstripes bags over there." She pointed to the stacks of bags across the room.

"What else?" Lydia asked, peering over Kiley's shoulder at the list.

"After that we tackle the other boxes. That's stuff that doesn't fit in the bags, and we're supposed to arrange it on the other tables. Might as well get started."

Kiley led the way to the tables and started unfolding them as Lydia looked at her with a strange grin.

"What?" Kiley asked.

"Or maybe we should go downstairs and listen to Audrey

143

rehearse her duet with Platinum," Lydia suggested. "Audrey'll take us with her to eat. Cuz that warm lemonade in the machine looks way too much like pee. Did I ever mention that the Amas drink sheep piss for certain ceremonies?"

The way Lydia's mind worked never failed to amaze Kiley. She saw a couple of box openers leaning against the wall, picked them up, and slapped one into Lydia's hand. "I'll do the tables. Go to work."

Unstacking all the tables, setting them up, and covering them with tablecloths was no easy task. Lydia actually joined in once she saw how tough it was, and Kiley was glad they'd both dressed down in official RMA staff T-shirts and jeans. Once the tables were set up, and the clothing racks rolled in, they set up a two-person assembly line with the boxes, walking down rows of the huge black and red bags and dropping one item at a time into them. Kiley took it in stride, but Lydia's eyes practically turned green as she parted with each item.

"A turquoise necklace by Fabulously Forty. A Swarovski crystal–embossed clutch purse from West Egg. A Bodog poker set. A certificate for a free cross-country flight on a private jet. Another certificate, this one for a free full set of Vera Bradley Signature luggage. Oh—look at this! A pink Cartier Tank Francaise watch."

"Is there a particular reason you're doing a play-by-play?" Kiley stuffed a portable cosmetic palette with the RMA logo created by Bobbi Brown just for this occasion into one of the bags.

"You think they'd notice if we took one of those?" There was longing in Lydia's voice.

"This is not your aunt's closet," Kiley pointed out. "You can't borrow a swag bag."

"I know." Lydia sighed. "Life is just not fair sometimes." She leaned against the table and picked up their instruction list, scanning the items they were supposedly going to find in the other boxes—the ones that wouldn't fit into the swag bags themselves. "Dang, Kiley, did you see all this other stuff? Shoes from Delman—they get to just pick what they want. Jeans made to order from paper denim and cloth. A motor-cycle jacket from Armani Collezioni—"

Kiley folded another gift certificate into a bag. "You might want to go look up 'covet' in the dictionary."

"Well, if you found my picture next to it, I'd be proud," Lydia said, holding one of the Cartier watches against her wrist. "And God bless America."

Kiley took a swig of water, then held the bottle to her face. The room was hot; evidently no one felt the need to turn on the air-conditioning for the worker ants. She looked over at the sea of boxes they had yet to unpack. "We need more help."

"Esme," Lydia said absentmindedly, admiring the clutch purse.

"More than Esme, I mean. Like six more people or we'll be here all night. That doesn't mean I'm not worried about her."

"Her parents, you mean," Lydia clarified. "You'd think someone with as much money and power as Steven Goldhagen could protect them, wouldn't you?"

"I know you think money and power fixes everything, but it really doesn't."

"*Almost* everything, and might I add that you are in a real snotty mood, girlfriend. Missing Tom?"

"Yeah," Kiley admitted. "But I don't think Tom's missing me."

She hadn't intended to get into it with her friends, because she didn't want to sound weenie and insecure, even if she *felt* weenie and insecure. But now that the subject had been broached, she couldn't avoid it. If she did, Lydia would just wear her down.

She filled Lydia in on the photos Matt had shown her of Marym and Tom kissing in Moscow. "I can't compete with a supermodel," she concluded.

Lydia idly wrapped a Chanel chain belt through her belt loops. "Now, see, you always do this—put yourself down. If Tom wanted to be with another girl, he'd be with another girl."

"He *is* with another girl," Kiley exclaimed, hurt coloring her voice. "That's the whole point! And put that belt back."

Lydia reluctantly took the belt off and added it to a swag bag. "Maybe that was just an 'Oh, hi' kind of kiss."

Kiley dead-eyed her. "Like I can't tell the difference between that and the real thing?"

Lydia considered. "Well, you could text Tom and ask him about it."

"There is no way—" Kiley began, but she never got to finish, because Lydia had spied Esme walking in and was already crossing the room to greet their friend in her usual exuberant fashion. "We're so glad to see you, sweet pea!" Lydia exclaimed, enveloping Esme in a bear hug.

Kiley joined them. She saw the fear and sadness in Esme's eyes, something that no hug was going to cure.

"What happened?" she asked quietly.

"It's terrible," Esme replied. Tears formed in the corners of her eyes. "My parents are gone."

An hour later, Kiley was sitting with Esme and Lydia on a yellow and white couch in the hospitality suite at Shutters on the Beach. Many of the out-of-town stars for the RMAs were staying at the very beautiful and very upscale hotel on the beach in Santa Monica. Because of that, there was a hospitality suite on the third floor, with a balcony overlooking the pristine beach and azure ocean. They'd called Steven beforehand and he'd told them they could finish up the swag room later. As long as it was done by the end of the day, there'd be no problem.

The hospitality suite was a penthouse hotel suite turned into a low-key, high-end hangout. It featured a table laden with gourmet food—jumbo prawns, lobster salad, rack of lamb—and a chef to oversee it. But the girls passed on the food and took only coffee. Since almost everyone was at the theater for rehearsal, the suite was nearly empty.

Esme brought them all up to date. Her ex, Junior, was essentially arranging for a "coyote" to smuggle her parents back into Mexico. It had to be done that way because if her parents were caught, they would never be allowed to immigrate legally.

"But as long as they're not caught, they can apply to come back?" Kiley asked hopefully.

"They can apply," Esme told her. "But a guy I know in the Echo who was born here? It took his parents six years before they could come. The shortest wait I ever heard of is nearly three years. There's a lot of people who want to come to

America, Kiley. Think about it. When someone's looking to get out of Nigeria, or the Philippines, you think they try to get into Cuba? No. They want to come here."

"I kind of know what it feels like," Lydia said softly. "I mean, my mom was just here. But I missed her as soon as she left. I don't know when she'll get back here. And my dad?"

Lydia sounded so sad that Kiley swallowed down a lump in her own throat. When she thought about the situation both her friends were in, separated from their parents by international borders, she felt selfish and self-indulgent for moaning about Tom and whom he might or might not be kissing. Yes, she certainly had issues with her own parents—especially her father when he hit the bottle. But to *know* she couldn't see them even if she wanted to? That would be really, really hard.

"You can go to Mexico and visit, can't you?" Kiley asked Esme.

"Yes." Esme stared into her coffee as if reading tea leaves. "But it's not the same. They won't be a part of my life here. I could get married, and they wouldn't even be able to come to my wedding. Now that *La Migra* has their photos, they'd be too afraid." She looked up. "Steven Goldhagen is being so wonderful, I can't even tell you. He says he's going to get my parents jobs at one of those upscale resorts where Americans go on vacation. He's got a friend who owns one in Puerto Vallarta."

"I'm seeing all three of us there for a vacation!" Lydia exclaimed. "How fun would that be?"

"And I'm making enough money to fly down to see them," Esme added.

"See? Your tattoo business is smart," Lydia told her.

"I don't have to pay if I don't want to," Esme said. "Steven and Diane said they're good for a ticket every two months."

Kiley was impressed. "You work for a saint."

Esme nearly smiled. "Steven would tell you that Jews don't have saints, but you're right. He is a wonderful man."

"You think he's doing it because you were seeing his son?" Lydia wondered.

"Not hardly," Esme replied. "For one thing, Jonathan and I are long over. I don't know what we are anymore. He's doing it out of regard for my parents."

Lydia lifted her sandal-clad foot and nudged Esme's shin. "And you, sweet pea."

"There is a catch. A big one," Esme said.

For the life of her, Kiley could not think of what it could be. "What is it?"

Esme set her coffee cup on the pale blue and daffodil yellow mosaic coffee table. "You know how my parents were so against me dropping out of school? Even though I'm making all this money?"

Kiley nodded. Frankly, she'd been against it, too.

"Well, Steven says the whole deal is predicated on my graduating. Because it's what my parents want for me."

"What about Esme Ink? Your business?" Lydia asked.

"At first I was thinking I'd have to close it down. If I decide to go to school, that is. But then Jorge suggested I hire some other tat artists and only work there for really big clients. Maybe even raise my rates."

Kiley fiddled with the small silver stud in her right ear. "I think it's a fantastic plan."

"But you like school, honey lamb," Lydia pointed out. "You're a freak of nature."

Kiley laughed. "It's a means to an end, so I take it seriously. That's what it would be for Esme, too."

Esme sighed. "With what I'm making on tats, I could afford to fly myself to visit my parents."

Kiley looked intently at her friend. "What are you going to do?"

Esme's eyes narrowed. "You know I hate being told what to do."

"But *he's* not telling you what to do, he's telling you what your *parents* would want you to do."

Before Kiley could say more, her cell rang. She checked caller ID, and her heart jumped.

"It's Tom," she told her friends. "I'm sorry to interrupt this, Esme, but he's calling from Russia."

Esme waved a hand. "Go take it. I'm fine."

"I won't be on long." She flipped her phone open and moved away from her friends into one of the empty bedrooms of the suite.

"Hello?" She sat on a canopy bed swathed in white fishnet.

"Hey, it's Tom!"

His voice sounded as if he was in the next room, as if she could round the corner and slide into his arms.

Kiley suddenly felt shy. "Hi. What time is it there?"

"Eleven hours later than where you are," Tom said.

Like she cared. She didn't even know why she'd asked that. Just for something to say that wasn't *Why were you kissing Marym?*

"So, how are you?" she asked, going for casual. Surely he

would just come right out and tell her about the kiss. He'd explain the whole thing, and then she wouldn't worry anymore.

"Great," Tom said. "I've finally got cell service. Russia is amazing. Being in Moscow is like being in Paris—very modern, lots of cafés."

"That's nice. How's the movie going?"

"They're having some problems with the financing," Tom said. "I don't know what, I don't really get into it. Chloë told me it happens all the time."

Chloë. That would be Chloë Sevigny. His new best friend.

"The Russian actors and the crew are fantastic. My stand-in has been teaching me this card game everyone plays here called *durak;* it means 'the fool.' The object of the game is to make one person lose and then laugh at them."

Kiley frowned. "That's just mean."

"Nah, it's just really Russian. You'd kind of have to be here to understand. So what's up with you?"

"School, the kids, and working on the Rock Music Awards with Esme and Lydia." She considered filling him in on Esme's troubles, but figured it would be better to wait until he got home. Then she considered telling him about her new friendship with Matt. But for some reason, she didn't. Maybe Tom would think she was just doing it to try and make him jealous. And he'd use it as a way to rationalize more kissy face with Miss Israeli Supermodel.

They chatted a while longer. He said he missed her, but Kiley could tell his heart wasn't in it. And he never mentioned Marym.

16

"I'm fagged out, ducks," Audrey told Lydia as she pulled her T-shirt over her head. She had already flung off her skinny jeans by the side of Kat's pool.

The pool area itself was lit by cool blue lights, both underwater and surrounding the terrace. Lydia watched as Audrey, clad only in her black lingerie, made a smooth dive into the deep end of the pool. Rehearsal at the Kodak had lasted until nine due to some technical glitches with the sound system. Even so, Lydia wondered how rehearsing a duet with Platinum could "fag" a person out.

"I could call the cook and ask her to make us something," Lydia offered. She sat by the side of the pool and ran her bare feet through the water, admiring the shocking pink polish on her toes.

Audrey treaded water, her tattooed arms colorful in the blue light. "Oh, no worries, Britney's bringing her chef."

Lydia frowned. They hadn't invited anyone over, let alone someone named Britney. As to why this Britney person would be bringing her own chef, Lydia had no clue.

"Who's Britney? And who invited her?"

Audrey laughed. "Funny."

"No, seriously, who?"

Audrey reached the lip of the pool in the deep end and hung on. "*Britney* Britney. She's joining us, and a few of my mates. Didn't I tell you? Maybe not. Sorry."

It was more than maybe not. Audrey had told Lydia no such thing. Because certainly if Audrey had mentioned that she'd invited Britney and her chef over, Lydia would have remembered. Back when Lydia was swatting away flying ants and eating monkey meat, Britney had been the queen of the world, her perfect visage appearing in nearly every one of Lydia's coveted magazines on a regular basis.

Britney was coming to her house? That was impossible.

"Britney," Lydia repeated.

"Don't be shocked. We've been friends since her third CD."

"So, Britney Spears is coming over and her chef is coming, too." Lydia just liked saying it.

"Her, some others, just a simple drop-in. Grab me a towel, love? This treading water is getting old, and I'm too tired to swim."

Audrey clambered from the pool and reached for the fluffy yellow-and-white-striped towel Lydia tossed to her. A few mates? Mates had to mean other famous singers and musicians. Or maybe movie stars. They were all coming here? Yes. Lydia was ready to bust from excitement.

There were only two things on her mind as she waited for

Audrey to towel off. One: was there anyone other than Kiley, Esme, and Flipper that she should invite? And two: what should she wear?

Two hours later, Lydia learned what "a few of my mates" really meant.

Her aunt's property was swarming with beautiful people; the famous and the infamous, and friends of the same. Audrey still insisted she'd invited only a few of her good friends. Well, evidently those few people had told a few dozen others who had told a few dozen others, and so on, until Lydia found herself hosting the impromptu rock and roll party of the year.

Not that the details weren't well handled. Car Candy, an all-female valet service, had been hired to park the multiple Mercedes and Lamborghinis and Priuses of the attendees. Not only had Britney's chef shown up, she'd brought with her an entire staff to cook and serve, along with a portable kitchen that she set up just outside the glass double doors leading to the kitchen. There were six different kinds of hot wings, mini Kobe beef burgers, a Chinese buffet, and a table laden with cupcakes by Joy the Baker, the best in the city. Down near the pool, three bartenders served mojitos and cosmopolitans and whatever else anyone wanted, with top-shelf alcohol only.

For once, her outfit had not come from her aunt's closet. Instead, Audrey had loaned her a cute candy-striped bikini that tied at both hips and around her neck. There was even a little pocket over her right ass cheek in which she could carry her cell phone.

Lydia stood near the shallow end of the pool drinking her

third watermelon martini. One of Pink's backup dancers had given it to her, explaining that it was made with crushed watermelon and really was superb. The martinis were making her feel effervescent. This was so much danged fun.

The swimming pool itself was full of guests, many of whom were drunk or stoned or in some obviously altered state. Some wore bathing suits, many of the girls wore only their bikini bottoms, and a couple of really wasted girls who were making out with each other in the shallow end wore nothing at all. Music blasted from the sound system Kat and Anya had installed when they'd bought the place.

"Hey. You throw a hell of a party."

Flipper came up behind Lydia, snaked his arms around her waist, and presented her with a fresh watermelon martini. He took the old glass as she sipped.

"It just kind of happened," she admitted. "But it's amazing."

"Woo-hoo!" A huge, hairy, shirtless guy in jeans whom Lydia recognized as one of the techies for the RMA jumped into the deep end holding a small goldfish bowl, which meant there were now goldfish swimming around in her aunt's pool. Well, no harm done. Goldfish were in the carp family, and carp could survive in practically anything.

She took another sip of her drink. Yummy.

"Want some food?" Flipper offered.

"I'm good," Lydia told him. "You go. Try the miniburgers. They're to die for."

"Will do. You are something else, Lydia Chandler."

"Yeah, I really am," she teased.

He swatted her butt lightly, gave her a kiss, and took off for the bar. Lydia took a few more sips of her martini. They really were excellent. She reminded herself to get the mix from the bartenders.

"You shagging him, ducks?" Audrey asked, stumbling over to Lydia with a half-empty champagne bottle in her right hand.

"Shagging?" Lydia echoed.

"Doing him."

"Oh, you mean are Flipper and I having sex? Not yet. But I'll drink to that!" She hoisted her martini glass in Audrey's direction. "I might have sex with him soon. I don't have a lot of experience and I'm looking forward to kind of broadening my horizons." She took a long swallow of her drink.

Audrey threw her head back and laughed. "You kill me!"

She handed Lydia the champagne bottle and Lydia thought, *Why not?* She took the bottle with her free hand and took a swallow. She loved the feeling of the bubbles exploding in her mouth.

"You know, I was thinking about those mystical potions you told me about. The ones you brought back from the rain forest."

"What about 'em?"

"I never did get to try one," Audrey reminded her. "What better time than a party?"

"Well, see, they're not really party drugs. The Amas take that stuff as serious as a heart attack."

"But you're not an Ama," Audrey said, giving Lydia a loopy grin. "And neither am I."

Lydia was going to explain how the Amas used those powders when Platinum herself weaved her way over to them. She wore a white bathing suit with fishnet across her flat, faux-tanned stomach, and white snakeskin sandals with a three-inch heel. "Kick-ass party, friend of Kiley."

Lydia laughed and thanked her. Then she took another swallow of the champagne. How much had she had? Was she drunk? She wasn't sure. She felt a bit dizzy, actually.

Platinum slung an arm around Audrey's diminutive shoulders. "Our duet is fucking great," she slurred. "We should do an album together."

"Love to," Audrey agreed.

I am standing here while two music legends discuss doing an album together. This is really happening.

Platinum took the champagne from Lydia. "I'm not supposed to drink anymore," she mentioned, then upended the bottle and chugged. When it was empty, she flung it into the pool and stumbled off into the night.

"Remember to get me the powder," Audrey called over her shoulder as she headed after Platinum. "Be a mate, mate. I'm dying to try your stuff."

Lydia just waved, hoping Audrey would be so stoned on whatever it was she was already mixing with the champagne that she'd just forget all about it. She really was not comfortable giving out any Ama concoctions for recreational use. It was kind of sacrilegious. On the other hand, she wanted Audrey to stay her friend. Lydia's life had gotten so much more exciting since Audrey had latched on to her. Plus, Audrey had bought her that incredible gown. She kind of owed the rock star. Didn't she?

Ah. There was Kiley. She was alone on the lawn, sitting in one of the wrought iron chairs, sipping what looked like a

Coke. Lydia headed for her friend, vaguely realizing that she was having a difficult time walking a straight line.

"How much have you had to drink?" Kiley asked.

"Don't recall. Going to bed alone, so I'm safe. I am crazed for watermelon martinis. Having fun?"

"I feel like I'm watching footage from TMZ or something on YouTube," Kiley confessed. "All these famous rock stars."

"I know." Lydia perched on the arm of Kiley's chair. "Audrey Birnbaum is livin' at *my house*. Just pinch me. Too bad Esme didn't come."

"I think rock stars and parties are pretty low on her priority list right now."

Lydia nodded. "I wish there was something we could do to cheer her up."

"Maybe we really could take a trip to Mexico with her sometime," Kiley mused. "That would be fun, huh?"

Lydia grinned. "And have sex on the beach."

"You want to have sex on the beach with who?" Kiley asked.

"It's a drink," Lydia explained. "Flipper says it's great. I might want to have sex on the beach with him sometime. I think he's probably good at it."

"Based on?"

Lydia stabbed a finger at her. "You know, you're right. I won't know if he's good at sex unless I actually have sex with him. There's a good reason for me to follow through. Should I change my mind about tonight?"

"I think you're kind of smashed, Lydia."

"Am I?" Lydia laughed and threw her arms in the air. "It's a party. You know, when Tom gets back, the four of us should go get rowdy. We could go dancing at the Silverbird Lounge."

"I don't even know if Tom is all that into me anymore," Kiley confessed.

"You're just havin' doubts cuz he's over there in Russia and you're here," Lydia insisted. She took the glass from Kiley's hand and took a sip. "Well, cut off my pinky and call me Betty. You're drinking too." Kiley's Coke was heavily laced with rum.

"One drink," Kiley admitted. She took her glass back. "I'm drowning my sorrows. At least I was trying to. It's not really working. And you might not want to mix rum and Coke with whatever else you were drinking. Hard on the stomach."

"What, sorrows about Tom?" Lydia questioned, ignoring the whole drinking lecture. She was having much too much fun to even think about it. "Have you not noticed that my not-so-humble abode is crawling with some of the hottest guys on the planet at this very moment? Reach out and grab you one!"

Kiley laughed. "How do you manage it?"

"What?"

"You never worry about anything," Kiley mused. "No matter what happens, you're always sure that you'll land on your feet."

"I have swung on vines over alligators and lived to tell the tale. That buoys up the old confidence about these things."

She stood, stumbling a little, but Kiley sprang up and righted her. "Thanks," Lydia said. "You're a great friend."

"You too."

Lydia took Kiley's hand. "Come on. We're gonna go find us some hotties and flirt!"

By the cool blue lights, Lydia saw two girls with immense fake breasts and tramp-stamp zodiac signs on their lower backs jump into the pool holding plates of food, which flew everywhere. "You're going to need the mother of all cleaning crews to clean this up," Kiley said, taking in the scene. "There's gotta be a hundred people here."

At that auspicious moment, Lydia's butt vibrated. It tickled so much that it made her laugh out loud. And then she finally realized—it was her cell phone. She checked caller ID but she was too drunk to make it out.

"What does that say?" She thrust the phone in front of Kiley.

"It says Kat Chandler. It's your aunt."

"Shit, shit, and double shit."

"Maybe you should just not answer," Kiley ventured.

"Right, good idea." Lydia felt the phone continue to vibrate in her palm. Finally it stopped. But not two seconds later, it vibrated again.

"She's not giving up," Lydia realized. "What time is it?"

Kiley squinted at the luminous hands of her watch. "Two-fifteen. She must think you're at home, in bed. And it must be an emergency for her to call you at two-fifteen in the morning."

They traded scared looks. Lydia couldn't decide what to do. Finally, she flipped her phone open.

"Hello?"

"Lydia, it's Kat. I'm so sorry to wake you—" She stopped midsentence. "What's all that noise?"

"Noise?" Lydia echoed, doing her best to sound sober. "It's, um, the TV! A movie. I couldn't sleep."

"Honey, you have school tomorrow, you need your rest,"

160

her aunt chided. "The only reason I called is that I've decided to drive back with the kids and I didn't want to scare you when we showed up."

"Driving back?"

"Impulse," her aunt continued. "The kids really miss home. Anyway, we should arrive around seven, before you leave for school. I just wanted you to know. See you then, sweetie."

"Great. Night. See you when you get here. In the morning."

She ended the call and stared wide-eyed at Kiley. Then she looked around at the hundred or so people trashing her aunt's property. There were another hundred or so people inside the house itself, doing who knew what, who knew where.

"My aunt will be home at seven," she told Kiley.

"Tomorrow night? You need to get that cleaning crew in here—"

"Tomorrow morning. I'm totally screwed, aren't I?"

Kiley nodded. "Pretty much."

"Okay, I'm not gonna panic. I just need to sit for a minute and figure this out." She flopped down onto the grass and lay on her back. There were a zillion stars in the night sky. All around her, people were still partying like there was no tomorrow.

Kiley knelt beside her. "I'd offer to tell everyone to leave, but I think we're way beyond that. And even if we could get everyone out of here, no way can we clean this place up in time."

"I know," Lydia agreed. She felt so dizzy. The stars were spinning above her. She closed her eyes.

"I'll figure something out, I will," she insisted. "Just give me a minute."

And that was the last thing Lydia remembered.

• • •

"Lydia! Lydia, sweetie!"

Someone was shaking Lydia's shoulder. She didn't want to wake up. She was having the greatest dream, naked on the beach with Flipper.

"Sweetie, you're going to be late for school!"

School? But she was at the party. Who was . . . ?

Holy hell fucking nightmare of her existence. It was her aunt Kat standing over her. Shaking her, calling her name.

It all came flooding back.

She was going to die.

She'd gotten wasted at the party. Hundreds of people trashing the property. Her aunt calling to say she'd be home with the kids. God. She was *so* screwed.

Lydia's eyes flew open.

To her shock, she was in her own bed in the guesthouse. Not out on the grass, as she remembered from the night before. She was in a T-shirt, not Audrey's bikini.

She looked around cautiously. Everything was in its place. There was even a vase with fresh flowers in it on the nightstand. How was that possible? How had she gotten undressed, into this T-shirt, and into bed? Surely her aunt had seen the destruction wrought by the night before on her way to the guesthouse.

Why didn't she sound mad?

"Hi," Lydia croaked cautiously. Her mouth felt as though it was full of cotton. Her head was hammering; her stomach felt as if it was going to revolt. It was a first-class A1 all-American hangover. It was terrible.

"The cook's got some eggs for you up at the house," Kat

162

said. "I'm so glad to be home." She gave Lydia a hug, which Lydia endured. Every inch of her flesh hurt.

"Great," Lydia replied. The mere thought of eggs made her want to hurl.

"Okay, I'll see you up there," Kat said, and started walking toward the door. Then she pivoted back.

"Thanks for taking such great care of the place while I was gone. Everything looks beautiful—and the fresh flowers everywhere—just so nice." She smiled at her niece. "It really means a lot to me."

Lydia fell back onto her pillow as her aunt departed. Maybe she was dreaming. That had to be it. Because none of this was making any sense.

Suddenly, Kiley's face appeared in the doorway. She was wearing what she'd worn the night before.

"Hi." She padded to Lydia's bed and sat on the edge.

"I have no clue what is going on. You slept over? The place is neat? There are fresh flowers everywhere?"

"After you passed out, I told Audrey your aunt was coming home. She made a few phone calls, had security clear the joint, and brought in the Rescue Crew."

"Who's the Rescue Crew? And do you have any Advil?"

Kiley smiled. "I'll get Advil. And coffee. The Rescue Crew was amazing. It's like a football team of cleaners, and not just the eleven on the field. They came in like an army at four in the morning and swept through this place, inside and out. You could eat off the floors."

"The swimming pool?" Lydia wondered.

"Perfect. Everything is perfect."

"Is Audrey here?"

Kiley shook her head. "When she heard your aunt was coming, she didn't want to mess things up for you. She went home with Platinum. Which is pretty funny—she's at my house, and I'm here. Anyway, that's the story."

"So except for my hangover—which feels like a million little people are stomping grapes in my head—I dodged a bullet?"

"Major bullet," Kiley agreed. "Which looked pretty damn undodgeable."

"Un-freaking-believable. I will tell my grandchildren about this one day."

"You'll also tell them that we actually got up and went to school," Kiley said, flinging back the covers. "I got you into bed, by the way. Now you have to get out of it."

Lydia put her bare feet on the cold wooden floor. "You're a great friend, Kiley."

"I kinda am. And the whole experience was kinda fantastic."

Lydia couldn't have said it better herself.

17

Esme watched and listened as Joe Satriani's fingers flew over his instrument. She had never heard anyone play guitar like this before.

Satriani was such an unlikely looking star. Bald, wearing dark sunglasses and a plain black T-shirt, he stood in the center of the Kodak Theatre stage without a microphone. He wasn't a singer; he was a pure guitarist whom Steven Goldhagen had selected to do the intros and outros to all the commercial breaks during broadcast. He would be situated off to one side of the stage, with his own camera and backdrop.

Now, as more than a hundred performers, camera people, crew people, and various hangers-on watched, Satriani was rehearsing the theme that he himself had composed for the show. It was vaguely Caribbean in feel, and so hooky that after five seconds you felt as if you'd heard it before and loved it.

It was the next morning. Esme had gotten to rehearsal

before Kiley and Lydia and had invited Jorge—he didn't have any classes until noon—to come and sit in, after getting Steven's okay. She glanced over at her friend, who watched Satriani play, his face rapt. Esme was glad he was enjoying himself. She, on the other hand, couldn't focus at all.

She kept thinking about her parents. She still hadn't heard from them. Junior had called her last night to say that he'd successfully dropped them off in Calexico as planned, and that his coyote there was prepared to sneak them across the border. However, he wanted to wait one more day, because the temperatures in the desert were close to a hundred and ten degrees, and the area of the border he wanted to cross offered no water and no shade.

The idea of her parents out there in the sun, with only what they could carry in their arms or in the coyote's backpack, was awful. How insane was it that her parents, citizens of Mexico, had to sneak back *into* Mexico? And what if they didn't have enough water? But Esme had heard on the news that another dozen people had been picked up by Immigration following the raid at Consolidated. Once you were deported to Mexico, you could never return to America. This way, at least, there was still a chance her parents could immigrate legally later on. Preserving that chance meant everything.

As Esme sat there in the Kodak, though, she found herself filled with dread. Had they really made the right decision? Maybe she should have counseled them to stay here in Los Angeles and just lie low for a while, until the frenzy had passed and they could resume their jobs, or find new ones. What would be worse—the fear of being taken into federal custody, or roasting to death under the blazing sun of the desert?

She sighed sadly. Both options had sucked. She'd feel a lot better when her folks contacted her. They had cell phones with plenty of minutes that had been unlocked for use south of the border. Why hadn't they called? Were they still in some part of the desert where there was no cellular service? That had to be it. But that would also mean they were exposed to the elements, trudging through the sand. Maybe they had to hunker down because the American border patrol had picked this particular day to enforce their particular area of the border. How hard would that be? Would the next call she got be from them in a holding cell?

The worst part was, there wasn't a damn thing that she, Jorge, the Goldhagens, or even Junior could do. They just had to wait and see. Esme hated to wait and see. She had never been a wait-and-see girl. It felt so passive. Just . . . wrong.

And then the idea hit her: she knew what she should have done. She should have gone with them. What an idiot she'd been! She was an American citizen. She could have crossed back to America simply by showing her passport. Her parents would have had her to guide them, to comfort them. Instead, they were out there alone, and here she was, in the Kodak Theatre watching a rehearsal.

How could she have been so selfish? Yes, they would have protested. Yes, they would have told her to stay in Los Angeles. Out of respect for them, she might even have agreed to let them go alone. But the right thing to do, after all they had sacrificed for her, was to offer. She hadn't even done that.

Suddenly, she couldn't sit there anymore, listening to the great music. Not while her parents were out there somewhere. She felt as if she couldn't breathe, and leaned toward Jorge. "I've got to get out of here."

Without waiting for him to say anything, she swiftly moved into the aisle and hustled out a side door that opened onto a tiled corridor; the corridor led back to the lobby. She heard, rather than saw, Jorge following her, but she didn't stop until she got to the long buffet table that held an assortment of refreshments. She cracked open an Arizona iced tea and drank.

"Nice escape," Jorge said as he sidled up next to her.

"I don't need your approval," she told him.

"Maybe not, but you could use my company."

"Maybe," she allowed, then looked around the lobby. Because it was just one day before the show, the producers had turned this area into a larger version of the greenroom to accommodate the many people that were now involved in rehearsals.

The buffet table held an assortment of pastries, bowls of fruit, and different kinds of wraps, plus coffee, tea, an espresso machine, and ten varieties of fresh fruit juices. Tables and chairs had been artfully arranged, along with potted palm trees and umbrellas, to add some ambiance. All this would be removed, Esme knew, in plenty of time for the show. But for now, it was like an on-scene counterpart to the hospitality suite at Shutters on the Beach, without the alcohol. It made sense. The social side of the Rock Music Awards was as important to the attendees as the awards themselves. After the show on Saturday, in fact, one of the parties would be right here in the lobby.

"You wish you could be with them," Jorge surmised.

"You a mind reader now?" Esme snapped, downing more of her iced tea.

"When it comes to you? Maybe."

It was true that no one knew her like Jorge. But sharing her feelings felt weak. And she refused to be weak. "I don't want to talk about it," she said.

"Which is why you need to talk about it," her friend answered.

"What I need is for them to get to Puerto Vallarta."

Jorge gazed at her for a moment, then rubbed his eyes wearily. "You drive me nuts, Esme. But in a good way. Go sit. I'll bring food."

Esme was about to protest, but then let her feet carry her to an empty round table with three bar stools. When she sagged onto one of them, she realized just how tired she was, and what a good sport Jorge was being. Who'd want to hang out with her at a time like this, except for a really good friend? Lydia and Kiley would be cool, of course. They were wonderful, and endlessly supportive. Yet she had a history with Jorge, and at a time of family crisis—there was no doubt that this was a family crisis—there was nothing like someone who knew you both then and now.

Junior was like that, and Jorge especially was like that. It was a blessing.

Jorge came back with a plate of thinly sliced mango, fresh strawberries, and pitted loquats. "Dig in."

"I'm not hungry."

He slid onto the stool next to her. "Fine. Then talk to me."

"There's nothing to talk about."

169

He smiled. "Then talk about the nothing in your heart. Hold on."

She raised her eyebrows as he took a small notebook out of his pocket, and a stub of pencil.

"Good line, might use it in a rap, gotta write it down." He scrawled quickly, then pocketed his notebook. "Okay. I'm all ears. Eat, talk, breathe. Choice is yours."

Esme didn't feel like eating. She didn't feel like talking, either, but she did anyway. She told Jorge about her fears for her parents, her guilt at not going with them, her larger guilt at being able to stay in America while they had to flee back to Mexico, and how she couldn't really sleep until she heard they were safe.

He took a mango slice and chewed it contemplatively. "What did they say to you?"

"What?"

"I know you, and I know your parents. Your mother is big on advice. I bet you asked for some before they left. What was it?"

Esme pursed her lips in frustration. She really did not want to have to share this, even though she knew she would. "They said . . . they said they wanted me to finish school."

"Ah." Jorge swallowed another piece of fruit.

"What does 'ah' mean?" Esme demanded. "Like you know so much?"

"I'm the guy who helped you open Esme Ink, remember?" Jorge pointed out. "But you know I agree with them."

The lobby hushed for a moment as the British rapper Petey Mac and American rocker Joe Leo swept in, then people started to buzz excitedly. Like Platinum and Audrey Birnbaum, they were slated to do a duet together.

"No one cares whether Petey Mac or Joe Leo finished high school," Esme said.

Jorge considered this. "Their parents might care. And if you had a chance to spend a day with me at UCLA, you'd care, too."

"Doubtful" was all Esme said.

"That's because you aren't even willing to give it a chance. Maybe you're afraid."

"I ain't afraid of anything. Or no one." Esme was getting pissed.

"I ain't so sure." Jorge echoed her phrasing on purpose. "I think you're afraid of maybe not being able to cut it. You're afraid you couldn't cut it at Bel Air High, and you're afraid that if you go to college, you won't be able to cut it there. So what if you were an honor student at Echo Park High? No one expects much from the poor brown kids. But what if you had to compete out in the real world?"

Esme's angry eyes flashed at him. Why was he being so pissy? "I need a friend, not a lecture."

"Academically, you can cut it against anyone," Jorge continued as if she'd never hurled her anger at him. "I know that. But you don't."

Esme was ready to scream. How dare he bust her chops like this, on a day like this? On the other hand, she knew who had been the first person she'd wanted to talk to when this crisis with her parents had erupted, and that Jorge's father would never, ever send a bill for the time and energy he'd put into her parents' case. She knew Jorge really cared. About her parents. About her.

"You're right," she finally said. "I don't."

His eyes shone. "You'll love college, if you ever decide to go. It's wonderful. Nothing like high school. Nothing. You take the classes you want, you find the professors you want. You find the people you want to hang with. And the best thing is, everyone wants to be there."

She nibbled on one of the strawberries. "Count me out, then."

"You think there's nothing you can learn? UCLA has a famous art department. You think the only canvas you can use is people's flesh?"

She dipped her pinky into some strawberry juice on her plate. "No." It had been a long, long time since Esme had done a sketch on paper, or dug out her cheap watercolor paints. She didn't even know where they were anymore.

Jorge put a hand on hers and looked into her eyes. "Just come with me. One day. That's all I ask." He hesitated a moment, then plunged on. "Think of how happy your mama and papa will be when you tell them, 'And I'm going to UCLA for a day with Jorge.'"

She had to smile at that. "You fight dirty."

"Say yes, Esme."

"No. You're manipulating me." She folded her arms defiantly, until he smiled at her with a goofy grin and a face he'd been making for several years that always cracked her up, no matter how much she tried not to laugh.

She laughed.

"Okay! Okay! I'll spend a day at UCLA just to get you off my ass. I'm going to the ladies'." When she hopped off her stool and headed to the john, Jorge was grinning at her.

The ladies' lounge in the lobby of the Kodak was beautiful. A wall of mirrors was decked by a marble vanity with all manner of mini toiletries nestled in small bamboo baskets—perfume, deodorant, mouthwash, hairspray, and lipstick. Esme noted they were all made by one of the huge companies that was sponsoring the Rock Music Awards.

Everyone had an angle.

She checked out her reflection in the mirror, fluffed her hair, tried one of the vials of perfume and liked it, then slicked on a tiny tube of lip gloss and stuck it in her pocket—the sample sizes were meant to be taken. Who was the girl she was staring at in the mirror, she wondered. Was Jorge right? Was she afraid to compete? If that was true, she didn't like what it said about her at all. It was not how she saw herself. And it wasn't who she wanted to be.

When she'd finished in the ladies' room, she returned to Jorge in the lobby. "I'm going to think about what you said," she promised.

"Once you spend the day with me at UCLA, I think you'll have the answer to all your questions," Jorge predicted. "Hey, someone stopped by while you were in the john."

"Kiley?" Esme guessed.

"Jonathan Goldhagen. Said he was here to help his dad. He also said he saw us sitting together."

She shrugged. "So?"

"So, what's up with you two?" Jorge asked.

Esme shrugged again.

"Ah, well, now I understand," Jorge said with obvious sarcasm.

"You asking me do I still have feelings for him or if we're still together or what?" Esme demanded. "We're not together." She struggled to be honest. "He's not good for me," she continued, not meeting Jorge's eyes. "I don't like who I am with him. And I don't think that's going to change. But the feelings I had for him . . . they don't just go away."

"Yeah." Jorge sounded a bit wistful.

"What?"

"Nothing."

"What did he say?"

He shook his head. "Doesn't matter." He slid off his stool. "I've got a class at noon and—"

She put a hand on his arm, hard and strong under her fingers. "Don't even think about leaving until you tell me what he said."

Still, Jorge hesitated. Then, finally: "Just because he said it doesn't mean I believe it—"

"Would you just tell me already?" Esme demanded.

"Fine. Jonathan told me that he was watching us for a while, that it was clear you were into me, and that you were the greatest girl he'd ever met in his life, but he was pretty sure he'd lost you. He warned me not to blow it. Like there's anything to blow," he added with a nervous laugh. "Okay. Now I got to get to class, *esa*. See ya."

Before she could even formulate a response, he'd grabbed his backpack and hustled away.

18

Kiley parked Platinum's Mercedes CLK convertible in the gravel turnaround near her guesthouse and shut off the engine. She sat there a moment, trying to muster the energy to go into the house. She was still wearing the clothes she'd worn to Lydia's impromptu party the night before.

It had been surreal that morning, going with Lydia up to the main house, where there were fresh blueberry croissants, juice, and a pot of coffee waiting for them on the kitchen table. Lydia's aunt had been surprised to see Kiley but had greeted her warmly; how nice it was that Kiley had stayed over to keep Lydia company. Lydia must have gotten lonely, all alone on the huge property. Would Kiley like some coffee, some juice, a warm croissant?

Kiley had accepted all three. She sat there, sipping coffee, and watched Lydia give an Academy Award–worthy performance. You never would have known that the girl was hungover. Kat had gone on and on about how great the place looked. She had no idea that only hours earlier a few hundred revelers had turned her home and grounds into a mosh pit of rock and roll decadence. There was simply no trace of it left. None.

Kat had been very chatty; she'd had a great time with the kids, who were exhausted from traveling all night and had headed right upstairs to bed. Somehow Kat was energized about being home again, minus Anya. It was going to be a fresh start.

Lydia had managed to chitchat with her aunt as if all was normal. She even managed to down a croissant with her five cups of black coffee. That girl, Kiley decided, had an iron constitution.

Fortunately Serenity and Sid had stayed over at Platinum's agent's house the night before—they were friends with the agent's kids—so Kiley didn't need to be at Platinum's to drive them to school. Instead, she'd driven Lydia. Yep, just two friends driving off to high school, waving goodbye to Lydia's aunt Kat as they got into the Mercedes.

Totally, utterly surreal. Thank God for the Rescue Crew.

Somehow, Lydia had made it through the school day. She even ran track during gym class. Kiley was the one who felt like crap. She'd dragged herself through the day, spacing out so totally in her Shakespeare class that when the teacher asked her to expound on Banquo's character in *Macbeth*, she was unable to even remember who Banquo was.

"I hate my dress," Serenity announced.

Kiley looked up. Serenity was standing by the Mercedes with her hands on her nonexistent hips, scowling.

"Hello to you too," Kiley said, reaching into the backseat

for her backpack full of books she should be studying tonight. "How was school?"

"Did you even hear me? I *said* I hate my dress."

Kiley got out of the car and slung her frayed backpack over one shoulder. "What dress is that, Serenity?"

"The one that doodyhead Chanis picked out for me," Serenity said. "For the Rock Music Awards."

"First of all, since you don't like people to call *you* names, it's a good idea not to call other people names," Kiley began. "And second of all—"

"It's *purple*," Serenity spit. "Hannah says purple is totally out this season. When I showed her a picture of my dress online, she laughed."

Hannah was the agent's high-school-aged daughter. Serenity idolized her. Kiley could not imagine what would make the girl dis Serenity's dress like that.

"So you have to call that doodyhead—"

"Serenity!"

Serenity sighed dramatically and folded her arms. "*Fine*. Call Chanis. Tell her I want the yellow dress I tried on first. And make sure she doesn't mix that up with the yellow and white dress because that one looked like puke on a Pringle."

"Colorfully put," Kiley commented. "Fine. The yellow dress. I'll call Chanis." Kiley was so tired her eyes felt gritty. Maybe if she took a shower and lay down for just fifteen or twenty minutes, she could cope.

"I'm going to take a break," Kiley said. "And then I'll meet you in your room in about forty-five minutes. Okay?"

"So you're going back to the guesthouse?"

"Yep," Kiley said, starting to walk away.

"There's a surprise waiting," Serenity singsonged.

Surprise? Kiley winced. Great. Just great. What other torture could a third-grade girl have planned for her? Especially a third grader with resources?

"Your boyfriend is waiting for you!" Serenity burst out.

Okay, that made no sense *at all*.

Kiley stopped and swung around. "What are you talking about?"

"Tom?" Serenity said as if Kiley was completely clueless. "Mom said he could wait in your living room."

Kiley's heart hammered away. No. That couldn't be true. "Tom's in Russia shooting a movie," she said carefully.

"Not anymore!" Serenity declared gleefully. "He's in your living room. Right this very minute. Can I watch you guys kiss?"

He wore jeans and a blue skater shirt, and he was sitting on the chintz-covered couch in Kiley's living room leafing through a *Hollywood Reporter*.

Kiley gaped at him. She was wearing the same clothes as last night, and she hadn't even washed her hair. It seemed to her that fate must have been cracking up, sending her cheating boyfriend back to her unannounced when she looked and felt like shit.

He stood and smiled. "Surprise," he said softly.

Kiley let her backpack fall at her feet. "What are you doing here?" It wasn't the most gracious way to greet him; that she knew. But it was what flew out of her mouth.

"Remember I told you there was trouble with financing on the movie?" he began. "Well, they stopped paying the crew.

178

For the past three days they've been promising things would resolve, but they never did. So they pulled the plug."

Kiley felt dizzy with confusion. "You're saying they already spent millions of dollars and then they just . . . canceled?"

"Happens more often than you'd think. I thought about texting, but then I decided to surprise you." He moved over to her and smiled into her eyes. "Missed you," he said softly, and hugged her.

Missed her. Ha. That was rich. Well, she'd at least give him a chance to tell her about Marym. She moved out of his embrace. He looked confused. She walked to the couch and plopped down; he sat next to her. "So, how was it while you were there?"

"Russia's amazing," Tom said. "The history, the people, the food. But the film . . ." He shook his head. "They never should have started shooting."

"What'd you do for fun?" Kiley asked. *Say it,* she thought. *Just say it out loud. I hooked up with Marym. At least tell me the truth.*

Tom shrugged. "Hung out. Played cards with the crew. Did a lot of sightseeing when I had free time." His brows knit together. "Is something wrong?"

"I'm just tired."

He reached up and ran his knuckles softly against her cheek. She shivered. His touch had always done that to her. Well, too bad. It probably did that to Marym, too.

"You sure that's all?" he pressed.

"Sure."

"This isn't a good surprise? I thought you'd be glad to see me."

"I am." Her words sounded stiff and false, and she knew it. "It's just that I have to go do something for Serenity, and Sid needs help with his reading project, and Bruce needs to be picked up from his friend's house, and then I have all this homework. . . ."

"Got ya. Sorry, I just didn't think." He rose. She walked him to the door. "I'll call you later?"

Her eyes didn't meet his. "Okay."

"Okay. Well . . ." He leaned down to kiss her; she gave him a quick peck.

She saw the hurt in his eyes. Or maybe that was just what she wanted to see. Well, let him hurt. Let him cry her a river. He was a cheater and a liar, and she was not going to let him break her heart.

She watched him walk down the gravel path—it felt as if she was watching him walk away forever. No matter how angry she was, or what resolution she'd made, she felt her heart breaking anyway.

19

Jimmy and Martina were practically jumping out of their skin with excitement. And even Kat, who talked to more famous people in a month than most of the world did in a lifetime, was giddy with anticipation. As for Lydia, she was thrilled that she was able to engineer this meet and greet. Her new best friend was coming over to meet her relatives. In fact, it had been Audrey who'd proposed the idea, and then followed through on it with a quick cell phone call to Lydia that morning.

"We're breaking between three and six," Audrey had told her. The call had caught her between English and history classes. "I thought maybe I'd stop over and say hi to your aunt and cousins. You told me they were fans, right?"

"Fans" was an understatement. Now that Anya was out of the house, Jimmy and Martina's true characters were beginning to emerge. Anya had been such a taskmaster with them, which did have some positives. Compared to the Ama kids in Amazonia, most American kids were soft to the max and utterly un-self-sufficient. On the other hand, Anya's to-do lists and every-minute-of-the-day-preprogrammed approach to life gave her cousins high anxiety. They were constantly looking over their shoulders, worried that the Merry Matron of Moscow might be ready to berate them for doing x and not doing y.

With Anya gone, it was fascinating to see the kids come into their own. They'd started by decorating their rooms, which pre-split had all the charm of prison cells in a Siberian gulag. Jimmy, who was in seventh grade, had opted for a video games theme, with posters from RuneScape, Gears of War, Halo, and GTA. Martina, two years younger than her brother, revealed a secret rock and roll identity that Lydia hadn't known existed. There were posters for Green Day, the Beatles, Bowling for Soup, and the Disturbed. And best of all, there was something of a shrine to Audrey Birnbaum, including even more posters, plus photographs that Martina had printed off the Internet. It turned out that Jimmy was also an Audrey fan. Lydia learned this by hearing him singing Audrey's hit "Jump-start My Heart" in the shower the morning they came back from their trip to San Francisco.

Lydia couldn't not take advantage of an opportunity to score some points with Jimmy and Martina and make their day. When she told Audrey that her young cousins were big fans, Audrey insisted on coming over to meet them. She'd bring a whole bunch of gear, she said, that she'd be happy to sign personally. Lydia marveled at it. How cool was Audrey? First she bought Lydia the mad hot evening gown for Saturday night. Then she'd somehow managed to get rid of every trace of the wild party at Aunt Kat's. And now . . . now this. Truly amazing.

X had picked the kids up at school and hustled them home, and Audrey had called to say that her limo was on the way. Kat had the chef put together an after-school snack of cookies, milk, and a bowl of fruit. Martina and Jimmy were waiting at the kitchen table. Martina had on an Audrey concert T-shirt (a baggy T-shirt; despite her weight loss and increased self-confidence, she still hated having breasts—and in her case, large breasts—way before the other girls in her class) and jeans, while Jimmy wore a sleeveless Everlast gym shirt and long ghetto-style shorts. He was in his dressing-like-a-rap-star phase, and ended nearly every sentence with "you know what I'm sayin'?" like his favorite rap stars. Kat wore tennis clothes. She was going to hit in the afternoon with the Williams sisters.

At the sound of the front-gate buzzer indicating that Audrey's limo was here, both kids practically ran to the front door, which made Kat laugh.

"If they ever greeted me that enthusiastically, I'd know something was wrong," she cracked.

"I'll bring Audrey in to meet you," Lydia promised.

Her aunt winked. "Only if she brought me a signed T-shirt."

Lydia decided to hang back and give her cousins the thrill of opening the door to the rock star. She heard the doorbell ring and watched as the kids looked at each other, undecided as to who should do the honors. Finally, Jimmy swung the door open. There stood Audrey, a guitar case in each hand, wearing skinny black jeans and a black tank top that revealed her tattooed arms. Lydia watched, amused and touched.

"Hello there. I'm looking for Jimmy and Martina Chandler," Audrey told them.

"That's us," Martina managed. "I'm Martina."

"Duh," Jimmy muttered. "She could probably figure that out, you know what I'm sayin'? I'm Jimmy."

"Fantastic!" Audrey exclaimed. "I'm Audrey."

"We know," Martina whispered, wide-eyed. "Are you really our cousin Lydia's friend?"

"We're fab mates for sure," Audrey assured. "Now, are you going to invite me in, or are we going to hang out here at the door? Either works for me. I'm easy."

Lydia decided it was time for her to make her presence known. "Audrey? You made it!"

"Lydia! Give us a hug, ducks!" Audrey put down the guitars and threw her arms wide; Lydia enjoyed the moment—and the gaping jaws of her cousins—as she hugged Audrey warmly and at length.

"Thanks for saving my ass," Lydia whispered in Audrey's ear. "The party . . ."

"All's well that ends well," Audrey said cheerfully, and gave Lydia another squeeze before releasing her.

"We've got some snacks inside," Martina said helpfully.

"Well then. Let's go in and see what you've got," Audrey responded.

Audrey retrieved her guitars and led the way to the kitchen, where Kat rose to greet her warmly, the ease honed by years of television interviewing and commentating apparent. Then Kat turned to Lydia.

"Lydia, there's something I wanted to show you upstairs," she said.

For a moment, Lydia didn't understand what was so urgent. Then she got it. Kat was engineering a way for Audrey to spend some alone time with her kids. Lydia was impressed, because Audrey did have a reputation for being a party girl. "Got it," Lydia responded, and turned to her cousins. "You guys okay if we leave you for a while?"

"Yup," Jimmy answered for both of them.

"Thank you so much for arranging for them to meet their idol," Kat said on the way out.

"My pleasure," Lydia replied sweetly. "It's the least I could do, after y'all have been so wonderful to me."

"So how's school, Lydia? Getting used to Bel Air High?"

"I'm not real big on spending my whole day inside a building, to tell you the truth," Lydia admitted.

Kat smiled and ushered Lydia into her bedroom so that they could continue talking. "No vines to swing from, huh?" Kat sat on the green love seat under a picture window that overlooked the tennis court. She patted the space next to her for Lydia to sit too.

"I just want to tell you how proud I am of you," Kat began. "Leaving you here while I took the kids to San Francisco. You had a huge house and a driver at your disposal. You could have abused the privilege. But clearly you didn't. And you're doing such a great job with your cousins. That's why I'm giving you a raise."

"Really?"

"Really. An extra hundred dollars a week. You've earned it."

Lydia thanked her aunt profusely. She knew she should feel guilty, since she had, in fact, violated her aunt's trust. But all she felt was relieved that she hadn't gotten caught. She wasn't sure that said anything great about her character. But really, who had been hurt by her antics with Audrey? No one.

She studied her aunt's tanned, unlined face, her bright blue eyes shining. "You really are okay without Anya," Lydia realized.

"I am," Kat agreed. "She'll always be the other mother of our kids, so she'll always be in my life. But beyond that, I'm ready to move on."

"Good," Lydia said. "You deserve all the happiness in the world, Aunt Kat." She gave her aunt a quick hug, then went back downstairs to see how her cousins were doing with the superstar.

She heard guitar strumming and singing coming from the kitchen. Not just one voice, either. Three voices: Audrey's, Martina's, and Jimmy's. Lydia moved forward as stealthily as a hungry Ama stalking a wild boar. Finally, she saw Audrey with her acoustic guitar, leading the kids in "Jump-start My Heart." In fact, she was letting them sing the melody while she sang a gentle harmony in the background.

Lydia waited for the song to end, so as not to embarrass her cousins. "How's it going?" she asked as she stepped into the kitchen.

"It's going fantastic," Audrey exulted. "We've got a couple of junior rock and rollers here."

Jimmy and Martina beamed at the compliment.

"Alas, I can't stay longer. I've got to get back to rehearsal. Lydia's going to ride with me. You'll watch the awards on TV on Saturday night?"

"Definitely," Martina promised.

"For sure," Jimmy agreed.

"Well then, that's great. And it's been wonderful meeting you. I'm off like a dirty nappy." Audrey stood and hugged first Martina, then Jimmy. Then she headed for the door. "Come on, Lydia."

"Wait!" Martina exclaimed.

Audrey turned. "What?"

"You forgot your guitars!"

Audrey grinned. "I didn't forget them. And they're not mine. They're now yours. I'm giving them to you."

"But—but—but—" Martina sounded like a low-power outboard motor, while Jimmy just sat there, astonished.

"Crap. There's one thing I forgot." Audrey bounded over to the kids and whipped a Sharpie out of her pocket. Then, she signed each of the guitars with a flourish. "As a rule, I don't sign guitars. But if you look at me and my life, I'm proof that rules are meant to be broken. See you guys."

"I . . . uh . . . thanks, um, Audrey," Jimmy told her, wide-eyed. "You know what I'm sayin'?"

"Yeah. Thanks!" Martina gushed.

Yeah. Super-duper thanks, Lydia added silently. *You just made two kids' day. No, their week. No, their year. Audrey? You are awesome.*

Audrey's limo was as well equipped as a hotel room. In fact, it was nicer than some hotel rooms, and far quieter. There was a plasma television that was tuned to MTV2, a laptop, two white leather couches that Audrey said folded out to become beds, and a sound system, plus a refrigerator full of food, beer, and the ubiquitous Taittinger champagne that Audrey loved so much.

At the moment, Audrey was sprawled across one of the couches, and Lydia across the other. It was a short ride to the theater from Kat's estate—south through the winding streets of the Hollywood Hills to Sunset Boulevard, then east to Highland and north to the Kodak.

"Giving those guitars to my cousins. That was amazing," Lydia told her.

"Nothing to it," Audrey said modestly. "I quite like kiddies, as long as they belong to someone else," she added with a grin. "Care for a coldie?" She reached into the minifridge and pulled out a beer.

Lydia shook her head. "No, thanks."

Audrey popped the top and took a long swallow. "I've had a blast staying at your place, ducks. So much better than some stuffy hotel."

"I'm sorry it had to end," Lydia said. "But now that my aunt and the kids are back . . ."

"No worries," Audrey insisted. "I'm leaving on tour in a few days anyhow. Five cities in Europe, then five cities in Asia."

"Seeing the world, staying in five-star hotels, screaming fans . . . sounds like a dream," Lydia said wistfully.

Audrey ran her thumbnail under the label on the beer bottle. "Actually it gets damn lonely." She grinned. "Now there's a bloody cliché for you, eh? Superstar on tour, surrounded by people, admits that she's lonely."

Lydia peered out the dark glass window—she could see out, but no one could see in. They were stuck in a traffic jam just down the street from the Kodak Theatre. Outside the window, she saw Grauman's Chinese Theatre. As usual, the street was full of tourists and eccentrics. There was a man on stilts in an Uncle Sam constume; another in black leather chaps, shirtless, with pierced nipples connected by a silver chain. A gaggle of Asian tourists was snapping his photo.

Audrey reached into the minifridge for another beer.

"It doesn't bother you to drink before you go onstage?" Lydia asked.

"Nothing bothers me," Audrey maintained. "I've got the constitution of a moose." She took a drink from the bottle. "So, love, I was thinking. About my tour. What would make it so much more fun is . . . if you came with."

Lydia wasn't sure she'd heard right. "Did you say . . . say it again."

"I'm inviting you to come on tour with me."

"But . . . what would my job be?"

Audrey laughed between swallows of beer. "No job, ducks. Just to hang out, have fun, make sure I have a few laughs. I'd pay for everything, of course. You'd get to see the world, and the inside of all those five-star hotels you were talking about."

"I have a job," Lydia reminded her. "And I'm still in high school."

"Yeah, well, if that's what you want. But you struck me as a free spirit. Kindred sisters. All that." The rock star's eyes bored into her own. "C'mon. I could use the company."

Whoa. Did she care about Bel Air High? Hell, no. She skipped school more than she went, and she didn't really care

189

about going to college, so she couldn't see how it mattered much. As far as taking care of her cousins, another nanny could do the job for a while. Surely Aunt Kat would understand. Surely she wouldn't begrudge Lydia taking the opportunity of a lifetime. . . .

"But if you can't, you can't," Audrey concluded.

"Hold up," Lydia said. "Who said I can't?" She knew it was impulsive. But if you weren't impulsive when you were a high school senior, when would you ever be? The day she turned down an offer like that was the day she had to turn herself in to the psych ward. She threw her arms around Audrey. "When do we leave?"

20

As Friday night slipped into Saturday morning, and the moon rose high in the Los Angeles sky, Esme couldn't sleep. In fact, she didn't even try. Her parents had been incommunicado since Wednesday, even though Junior had reported that the transfer in Calexico to the coyote had gone without a hitch. Esme knew they wouldn't try to cross the border there, to Mexicali on the other side. Instead, they'd be taken out into the desert, past the new security fence between the United States and its neighbor to the south. There, they'd play a cat-and-mouse game with the border patrol under the guidance of their coyote, waiting for a propitious moment to cross southward.

That fence made things infinitely more complicated. Yes, the saying was that if you find a fifteen-foot wall, you just need a sixteen-foot ladder to get over it. On the other hand, you'd be sixteen feet up, there'd be no ladder on the other side, and you still had to get the damn ladder to the fence in the first place. Plus there were helicopters, jeeps, and cameras. Just to get back into Mexico without getting caught. Loco.

She'd called everyone. Junior had done his best to reassure her. So had Jorge and his father. Steven and Diane had told her to take the night off, that Diane would watch the girls while Steven was at rehearsal for the show. Esme thought that was a good thing—the twins still didn't spend much time with their mother unless someone else was there to help. Esme appreciated that all these people cared and were trying to look out for her. But the inactivity was worse than being busy. She'd even rescheduled a tattoo for the drummer of a band that currently had the number-two CD in the country, because she didn't feel she could concentrate well enough to do her best. Instead, she'd gone online to pass the time, and found herself eating pistachios and reading firsthand accounts of harrowing border crossings, and newspaper stories about the border fence and heightened security. It made her so sick to her stomach that she knew she should quit. But somehow she couldn't.

It was when she was going to her cupboard for her third helping of pistachios—even though her stomach was saying she'd eaten more than enough already—that her cell rang. Caller ID was restricted, but she still opened it breathlessly. Maybe, just maybe . . .

Please, let it be my parents.

"Hello?"

"*Hola, Esme, Papa aquí.*"

Hello, Esme, it's your father. Esme nearly fell over with relief.

Tears streamed down her cheeks, and she made no effort to wipe them away.

"Are you safe? Papa, are you safe?"

Her father's words were comforting. "We're in Mexico. We're safe. We weren't safe for a long time in the crossing, but we are safe now."

"Mama, too?"

She heard her mother's voice in the background, in English. "Hi, beautiful daughter! It's your mother!"

Now, she finally relaxed, stepping over into her bedroom and sagging onto the red antique quilt. Her muscles ached—every muscle ached. She realized how tense they had been for the last day and a half.

"Where are you? Why did it take so long for you to call me? What happened?"

"I'll let your mother tell you. No matter what she tells you, know that we are fine now." Her father was emphatic.

She heard her father give her mother the phone, and then listened in stunned silence as her mother told the tale of how they crossed the border. For whatever reason, the coyote had led them into an area swarming with border patrol. They'd had to hide out in a crude cave for all of Wednesday night and half of Thursday. Their water had run short, and there were scorpions. They could hear the helicopters and jeeps in the desert, and even loudspeakers telling any illegals in the desert to freeze where they were.

"They were looking for people coming from Mexico to America," her mother said. "But that didn't mean they would not have swept us up, too."

"I should have been with you," Esme exclaimed, still regretting that she hadn't thought of this before they'd left.

"Your papa never would have let you come, *m'ija*. And there was room in the cave for only three people," her mother explained. "If you had come we could not have hid there and we would have been captured."

Esme had no idea if this was true or if her mother was just saying it to make her feel better. And she never would know, because neither parent would ever tell her.

For Estella Castaneda, that was a long speech. But the upshot of it was clear. Estella was reminding Esme of her parting words on Wednesday, when she and Esme's father had told Esme they wanted her to finish high school. Esme understood. *Sometimes your mother knows things that you do not.* She understood, but wasn't sure she agreed. No matter what, this wasn't the time or place to launch into that discussion.

"What's next?" Esme asked.

"We go to Puerto Vallarta," her mother replied. "We should be there soon. I hope that we can start work at the resort on Monday. We will send Steven and Diane a letter of thanks. But I want you to thank them again for us in person. Will you do that?"

"Of course, Mama."

"And what about you, *mi estimada*?"

Esme knew what her mother meant—was Esme going back to school as her parents wanted. She sidestepped the implied question and simply assured her mother that she was fine.

The conversation went on a while longer—it was hard for Esme to say goodbye. Finally, with the promise of another phone call on Sunday, Estella said they had to get going—they wanted to sleep in a real bed this evening instead of under the stars on a "mattress" made of endless sand.

"Goodbye, Mama."

"Goodbye, *querida*. Make good choices."

That was it. The call went dead in Esme's hand. *Make good choices.* But what if what Esme thought was a good choice for her was not her mother's choice? She had no answer to that. Still, she was overcome with relief just to know that her parents were all right.

Tomorrow night was the Rock Music Awards, and Esme knew her day would be insane. But even though it was after one, there was no way she could sleep. She knew she shouldn't call anyone that late, but . . .

She called Kiley, then Lydia, and quickly gave them the great news about her parents. They were, of course, delighted. Then she hung up and called Jorge. He was up reading the end of John Edgar Wideman's *Philadelphia Fire*, which had been assigned in his freshman literature class.

"It's great news, Esme," he told her softly. "I guess Junior came through for you."

Jorge had never been a fan of Junior's, had always thought his best friend could and should do better than a high school dropout and former gangbanger.

"Yes, he came through for me," she agreed. "And for my parents."

"I'll tell my father first thing in the morning," Jorge promised. "He'll be happy."

"I guess it's too late to go out. I'm too jazzed to sleep so I thought maybe . . ."

195

She left the rest of the question unsaid. There was silence on the other end of the phone. Esme could feel the heat rush to her face.

Finally, after what felt like forever: "Esme, you askin' me out?"

"Yes, I'm asking you out," she confirmed.

"Like on a date?"

"Yeah," she mumbled.

"A friend date or a date-date? Because I need some clarification here."

"Depends," Esme began, because there was only so far she was willing to stick her neck out. "You want it to be a date-date?"

"Oh no, I'm not letting you get away with that. You asked. You decide."

She exhaled slowly. "Fine. A *date*-date. You happy now?"

She felt as if she could hear his smile over the phone. "Yeah. I'm happy."

They agreed to meet at Hector's, a new club in Los Feliz that stayed open until three. Jorge had a friend who worked there.

Esme hung up and stared at her phone. She was going on a date with her best friend. That could ruin everything.

She left her car with the valet on Los Feliz Boulevard and walked into Hector's. It was cozy, dimly lit, and still full of patrons even though the neon wall clock said it was 2:15 in the morning. A bar with orange and pink leopard-print stools ran the length of the rear wall. Midnight blue velvet love seats were placed in dark corners here and there. On a small stage near the front, a lone guitarist played classic Spanish love songs.

She was relieved to see that Jorge had arrived before she did.

"Hello," he said softly as he approached her in the doorway.

He wore a blue button-down shirt untucked under a khaki cotton blazer Esme had never seen before, and jeans. Back at her guesthouse, flying on the good news of her parents' safe arrival in Mexico, Esme had put on a short, tight black skirt and very high heels. But just before leaving, she decided it felt ridiculous to meet Jorge in such a getup. That was the kind of outfit Junior had loved. He'd loved for all the men, no matter where they were, to look at her and to know that she was all his.

With Jonathan, she'd also changed her style. She made an effort to dress classy, to fit in with his rich, white show-business friends. But with Jorge, she knew she didn't have to put on any kind of artifice. He'd see right through it, and then call her on it. So she'd changed into jeans and a magenta cotton sweater that was neither tight nor low-cut. It felt right.

"I got us a table," Jorge said, and led her to a love seat nestled in a corner. The table already held a pitcher of something dark and two glasses.

"Dark beer?" she guessed, settling onto the love seat.

"Coke." Jorge chuckled and poured her a glassful. "But if you wanted to get me drunk you should have just said so. There's plenty to celebrate. Like you being here with me, for instance."

Esme was embarrassed. "Very funny." This was so weird. She *never* felt embarrassed with Jorge.

She lifted her glass and clinked it against his. "Here's to my parents."

"To your parents," Jorge echoed, and took a sip. He asked if Esme was hungry, and she realized she was starving. Hector's specialized in Cuban food, so they ordered a few different octopus appetizers from a beautiful waitress with skin the color of burnished copper, her hair slicked back in a long ponytail, a Cuban flag pin on her lapel. Esme wondered idly if a waitress in Havana could get away with an American flag pin on her uniform. Probably not, she decided.

When the waitress moved off, Esme ran her forefinger around the rim of her glass. "The last thing my mother said to me was 'make good choices.' That's code."

Jorge nodded. "For finishing school and going to college."

"But I still don't see the point," Esme insisted. It was easy to remember the faces of those mean, privileged girls who had shown her and Kiley and Lydia around Bel Air High on the first day. As if they were so superior. So much better than her.

"I've got a business that's making good money. More than I could even with a college degree. So no way am I going to torture myself at Bel Air High School. And I'm not finishing high school in Echo Park, either," she added vehemently. "I've had enough of that place, too."

That was true. Yes, the Echo would always be part of her. But the idea of surrounding herself again with her past was too much to swallow.

Jorge raised his eyebrows. "Fair enough. Okay, so you find another way. You want to get somewhere and you reach a roadblock, you find a way to go around it. Because I know you. You think roadblocks are for other people." He put an arm around the back of the love seat, close to her shoulder. "I need to ask you something."

"What?"

"You and Jonathan," Jorge said. "What's up with that?"

She shrugged.

"That's not an answer."

Jorge sounded annoyed and, Esme realized, he looked it too. He leaned toward her, his dark eyes holding hers, and withdrew his arm from where he'd draped it. "If you're still seeing him, even maybe seeing him, then you aren't seeing me, and this is not a date."

Esme was saved from having to answer that question quickly when the waitress came back with their appetizers. There was coconut octopus with a dipping sauce, fried octopus, and a cold octopus ceviche. She reached for a piece of the fried octopus and snared it with two fingers. It was her turn to be annoyed. What difference did it make, really, if she decided she still wanted to see Jonathan?

"You don't hear me asking you who you're seeing at UCLA." She popped the octopus into her mouth and chewed. Pretty good. In fact, really good.

"I'm not playing that game," Jorge said flatly. "And if you don't know the answer to my question, then this is not a date." He folded his arms. Esme put her hand on one of them.

"Come on, don't be like that."

"Like what? I'm not playing games with you. If I'm seeing you now, that should answer your question about UCLA. I'm not seeing anyone there, and it's not for lack of opportunity, either. If you're seeing Jonathan—"

"I'm not! Happy?"

He ate a piece of octopus himself before commenting with a soft smile, "Why was it so hard for you to say that?"

Good question. Jonathan had hurt her in some profound way. She never wanted to hurt like that again, or to feel that needy.

"Love shouldn't hurt," she finally told him. "But with him, it hurt. I tried so hard to be what he wanted. And then I hated myself for it."

For the second time that night, she felt hot tears coming to her eyes. This time, she brushed them away angrily. She did *not* cry in public, dammit. Ever.

Jorge stood and held a hand out to her. *"Quieres bailar conmigo?"*

Esme looked at the small dance floor in front of the stage. It was empty. "No one else is dancing," she protested.

"Since when do you care what everyone else does?" His hand was still extended toward her.

She took his hand. They moved to the dance floor and she went into Jorge's arms. He wasn't nearly as tall as Jonathan, or as muscular. He didn't exude money and power. Every girl in the place was not watching him and lusting after him. And yet . . . his arms felt strong and sure around her.

Still, this was dangerous. What if she lost his friendship? Esme didn't think she could bear that. It was nearly enough for her to go sit back down and make jokes and push him away.

She was just about to do it when he whispered her name into her thick, lustrous hair. "Esme."

"Yes?"

"Just Esme."

Was she willing to risk everything? Was she willing to trust him?

As if her body knew the answer better than her heart, Esme's eyes closed, and she moved closer into his embrace. It felt like coming home.

21

"Y'all, how cool is this, our own dressing room!" Lydia exclaimed to Esme and Kiley as she slicked a wand of baby pink lip gloss over her full lips. "We really should have our names on the door, though."

It was Saturday afternoon, and the Rock Music Awards would start in an hour. Lydia was so excited she felt as if she could fly. At the final run-through, Steven Goldhagen told them they would be the ones who escorted the winners from the stage after they made their thank-you speeches. It had merited them their own small dressing room under the Kodak Theatre.

Lydia already had an amazing gown, thanks to Audrey. The stylist for the awards had found gowns for Esme and Kiley, too, although they had to be returned the next day. Esme's was a red satin Escada, while Kiley had been fitted in a green silk chiffon by Marianne Lanting. Their hair and makeup had been done by one of the army of makeup artists ensconced in the theater's sub-basement. Now, they were just waiting for the signal from Jocelyn to come upstairs and take their places in the wings.

It did feel a little strange to be preparing for the awards at four in the afternoon—the show itself would start at five—but it all had to do with the vagaries of television. There would be a live broadcast to the rest of the country, and the producers didn't want to begin later than eight o'clock New York time. Viewers in the Eastern and Central time zones would be watching live; those in Mountain and Pacific would watch on tape delay. Awards shows were difficult enough to sell to viewers, because all a person had to do was log on from anywhere during the original broadcast to find out who won. There was lots of illegal streaming, too. Who would bother to watch on tape?

There was a video monitor in their dressing room showing a live feed from the red carpet area outside the theater. Huge crowds on both sides of the carpet cheered, snapped photos, and begged for autographs as the stars arrived for the show. Lydia had watched as Platinum and Audrey emerged arm in arm from a white limousine, Platinum in a white gown, Audrey in black. It seemed to Lydia that Audrey was weaving a bit as she and Platinum worked their way down the red carpet—probably too much champagne in the limo, she figured. Well, what the hell. This was the Rock Music Awards, not the Oscars. People expected the unexpected to happen.

This was great; in fact, everything was great. Things were even great with Esme's parents, who had safely arrived in Mexico. There was only one thing. Lydia hadn't yet informed Esme and Kiley that she was planning to stay in Los Angeles for only another couple of weeks, before she'd hook up with Audrey and travel with her on the world tour. She hadn't exactly informed her aunt Kat yet, either. Well, she for sure planned to find her aunt another nanny before she left, so that should take some of the sting out. She'd poach someone at the country club.

Of course, Audrey's tour would end eventually. What if Kat liked the sub nanny better than she liked Lydia? What if she decided to punish Lydia by not giving her the gig back?

Lydia waved a hand through the air as if to dismiss all the questions. No girl in her right mind would turn down touring with Audrey Birnbaum. So why was she still hesitating?

Maybe it had to do with her friends. She, Kiley, and Esme had stuck by each other all summer. They were like each other's families. Now, with Esme's mother and father back in Mexico, it would be even more so. It would be hard to tell them—very hard. And the longer she waited, the harder it would be.

"Esme? Kiley?" Lydia felt her heart beat faster. "Can we talk for a minute?"

Shit on a shrub—she'd said it. Now she had to follow through.

"Sure. What's up?" Kiley asked.

"You and Billy are back together?" Esme guessed.

"You know, I really, really care about that boy," Lydia said. "The problem is, if we were together, he wouldn't want me to be with anyone else."

Lydia saw Kiley and Esme exchange a look. "You are definitely not ready for a relationship," Kiley pronounced.

"So, what is it?" Esme pressed. "You going back to the Amazon?"

She just had to say it. Flat out. If her friends were really her friends, they'd want what was best for her.

"Well, see, Audrey's leaving on her world tour in like two weeks? She asked me to go with her. All expenses paid, as her friend. I said yes."

Dead silence, except for the voices of the producers in the booth filtering through the monitor.

Then, Kiley spoke. "Wow."

"You gotta be kidding." Esme was, as usual, blunter. "What about your life?"

"What about it?" Lydia responded. "Audrey and I have gotten really close, and she made me this incredible offer. Y'all, I may never get another chance like this in my entire life."

She continued making her case. She hated school. She'd be back in eight or nine months. She wouldn't have to spend a dime—Audrey would pay for everything. It was the opportunity of a lifetime.

"Wow," Kiley said again. "How can you not go?"

"Excuse me?" That was not the reaction Lydia had expected, especially from Kiley. "I thought you would give me a big ol' lecture about school and responsibility. If you were in my Manolos, would you go?"

"You already know," Esme said before Kiley could respond. "She wouldn't leave Tom."

"Well, see, that does not make sense, because Tom just left her to go to Russia," Lydia pointed out. "What's good for the goose and all that. Right, Kiley?"

Lydia thought she saw something sad flit across Kiley's face, Then it was gone.

Esme stood and moved some magazines off the vanity. "If you've given your heart away, it's not that easy. Where did I put my purse?"

Lydia found it under the chair and handed it to her.

"Thanks," Esme said. "Listen, I'm the last person to step on someone else's dreams, Lydia. But you might want to think about what it would be like to be completely dependent on Audrey. What if you have a fight? What if you don't feel like doing what she feels like doing?"

"It'll work out," Lydia insisted.

Kiley smiled at her. "We'll miss you."

"But we'll survive," Esme added. "Compared to what my parents just went through, our lives are cushy."

"I'll miss you guys, too." Lydia blinked back her sadness. It was one thing to talk about going on this trip in theory, and quite another to talk about it in practice. She felt homesick for her friends already.

Esme smiled. "It's not how it used to be. I can even talk to my folks in Mexico by Skype. You'll have a laptop. We won't forget you."

"And I won't forget you guys, either. I promise."

"There's something I need to tell you guys, too," Kiley said softly.

"You're going on tour with Platinum?" Lydia kidded. "Can you imagine what her bus was like back in the day? Man," she said, shaking her head. "I only hope Audrey and I can live up to that legacy."

Kiley licked her lips nervously. "What I wanted to tell you

guys is that I think Tom and I are over. He's back from Russia. They ran out of money on his movie."

Lydia sighed. Kiley had already mentioned the photographs she'd seen of Tom and Marym together in Russia, but she hadn't said that those pictures had led to her and Tom splitting up. If Kiley only had Lydia's attitude toward relationships, she wouldn't have that sad face right now.

"What happened?" Esme asked her.

They listened to Kiley explain what had happened with her new friend Matt. Tom and Marym had apparently hooked up in Moscow. On the one hand, Lydia wanted to tell her friend to buck up. That was Russia, this is America, and what happened during a movie shoot—even an aborted movie shoot—in Russia could well stay in Russia. The Amas in Brazil tended to take a more liberal point of view toward monogamy than Americans. Not that Kiley would care. Growing up in Wisconsin and growing up in the Amazon were two different things.

"Have you talked to him?" Lydia asked.

"On Thursday. But there wasn't much to say. It was . . . awkward. Those photographs didn't lie." Kiley was emphatic.

Esme nodded. "You need a guy who's there for you even when you're apart."

"Yeah," Kiley agreed. "I guess Tom isn't that guy."

Lydia saw a tear track down Kiley's cheek. "Oh, sweet pea, don't cry over him." She gave her a hug. "If he doesn't appreciate how fabulous you are, then he's over."

"But, he was the first guy I ever . . . you know," Kiley said, brushing the tear away. "And now I'm so sorry."

"I'll try and send you an Irish guy named Liam. Or a French guy named François. Or a German guy named Dirk.

Or an Ama guy. Naw. Let's pass on the Ama guy," Lydia cracked. "You like 'em with teeth."

Lydia saw that Kiley was about to retort, but then Jocelyn's voice came over the closed-circuit intercom system. "Lydia? You three ready?"

She bounded over to the intercom on the wall and pressed the Talk button. "Yeah, we're all here."

"Then get your asses upstairs. We've got a show to put on!"

That was it. It was time. The Rock Music Awards were about to begin.

Lydia and Kiley were stationed to the left side of the stage, while Esme was moved to the right. The Kodak auditorium was jammed. Many of the seats had been taken out and round tables brought in, at which the stars, their entourages, and media company executives were seated. Farther back were industry-related fans, while the two Kodak Theatre balconies were reserved for regular-human-being fans, including a goodly number who'd come from overseas. Tickets to the Rock Music Awards were a coveted giveaway premium for radio stations and magazines around the world, and lots of those regular fans had won their tickets and, in some cases, their trips. These fans in the upper deck were the loudest, cheering for their favorites.

The performances were incredible. John Mayer, Coldplay, the Pussycat Dolls, Usher, Fergie, the Killers, Kanye West—the list went on and on. Lydia was waiting for the presentation of the next award, a lifetime achievement award to Simon Cowell of *American Idol*. She would be the one escorting

Simon offstage. Right now, the video monitors in the theater were showing a lengthy retrospective of Simon's life, from his birth in Brighton, England, through his youth and his start in the music business at EMI and his work as a consultant at BMG. Then, the retrospective shifted to the hit TV show; there were video thank-yous from Ryan Seacrest, Paula, Randy and Kara together, and several American Idols of the past.

Lydia eased over toward Kiley, who was waiting to escort the winner of the Best Album award offstage. That would be presented by Platinum and Audrey after their duet. "How cool is this?"

"Cool. Unbelievable," Kiley whispered back.

"Cool enough to make you forget about Tom?"

Lydia saw in Kiley's eyes that the answer was no. "But I'm trying," Kiley promised.

"Excuse me?" A tall, model-thin girl with curly bright red hair and a matching sleeveless red dress, wearing high heels that made her tower over both Lydia and Kiley, stepped up to them.

"Yes?" Lydia asked. "Can I help you?"

"Your friend can help me," the girl replied. "She's Kiley McCann, right?"

"Right," Kiley responded. "Do I know you?"

"I'm Abbey Lee. I think you were at my engagement party. For me and my fiancé, Slade. At the bowling alley? With Matt, right?"

"Right," Kiley confirmed. "Nice party."

"And I saw you a while ago with Tom Chappelle," Abbey went on. "You guys are a couple?"

"We were," Kiley said.

Abbey fixed her gaze on Kiley and fiddled with the diamond pendant around her neck. "Look, I know this is none of my business. But I just wanted to tell you something about Matt. Warn you, actually. He's a good guy. One of the best. But he's gay. He has the hugest crush on Tom. So if that's the reason—"

"Your friend Matt is gay and has a crush on Tom?" Lydia interrupted, because she really wanted confirmation of what she'd just heard. It put a new spin on everything.

"Are you sure?" Kiley didn't seem to believe it.

"Oh yeah," Abbey insisted. "Everyone knows. Even Tom. Did you tell him you and Matt got to be friends?"

Lydia saw Kiley redden. "No," she admitted.

"Well, if Matt was talking trash about Tom to get you guys to split up? It wouldn't be the first time, that's all I'm saying," Abbey concluded. "I gotta go. Maybe I'll see you at the after-party." With that, she zipped away, as comfortable in her high heels as Lydia was in bare feet. Kiley stared after her, gape-mouthed, as Lydia chortled.

"He's gay! Matt's gay! Can you believe it?"

"And he has a crush on Tom," Kiley added. She sounded as though she was in shock.

Lydia took Kiley by the shoulders. "Those pictures that Matt showed you. Of Tom and Marym in Russia. Were they originals?"

"I don't know. I didn't have a reason to ask."

"Dang, I bet Matt cropped them, or Photoshopped them, or something like that," Lydia guessed. "He set you up so that you'd break up with Tom!"

Lydia would have said more, but the big announcement

came from the film director Quentin Tarantino, who was making the presentation to Simon. "And the Rock Music Lifetime Achievement Award goes to Simon Cowell!"

The theater erupted in applause, and then a standing ovation. Simon, who was wearing one of his trademark black-T-shirt-and-jeans outfits under a tux jacket, bounded up the aisle from the Fox Television table and onto the stage to even more applause.

"Are you planning on watching, or escorting?" Lydia heard Jocelyn's voice behind her.

"Escorting! I'm on it!" Lydia had been so taken in by the moment that she'd forgotten to go out onto the stage. But it wasn't a big problem. Simon soaked up the applause, and she made her way out in plenty of time for him to deliver a short acceptance speech and accept his guitar-shaped trophy. Then, she escorted him to the rear of the stage before the show went to Joe Satriani's solo and a preplanned commercial break.

The next segment of the show would be Audrey and Platinum's duet. They were due to enter from opposite sides of the stage. In fact, Audrey was standing backstage when Lydia came off with Simon, wearing a fitted black sleeveless gown by Patricia Field.

It took Lydia about twenty seconds to assess that Audrey was in no condition to perform.

"Pidia!" Audrey exclaimed. "How you be, ducks?"

"I be okay," Lydia answered cautiously.

"Fuck a duck!" Audrey gave a high-pitched giggle. Then she started singing to the tune of "Row, Row, Row Your Boat." *"Fuck, fuck, fuck your duck, gently down the stream!"*

"What are you taking?" Lydia asked carefully.

Audrey leaned her head close. "You have some awesome powder from the Amazon! I found it in your room. You want to do some of it with me, ducks?"

Audrey reached into her dress pocket and extracted a small baggie containing the blue-brown psychotropic powder Lydia had brought back from Amazonia. "This stuff is amazing. Totally amazing! It's better than any drug I've ever taken, and that's saying a lot. Woo-hoo! Woo-hoo! Woo-hoo!" She hooked her fingers under the bodice of her strapless gown and folded it downward, exposing her bare breasts. "The twins need some air!"

Audrey giggled like a crazy woman. Then she started dancing around as if she was hearing music in her own head. This in and of itself was not shocking; Lydia had seen Ama tribesmen do it many times under the influence of the same powder. However, none of the Ama tribesmen ever had to go out onto the stage of the Kodak Theatre and perform a duet in front of several thousand people, and a worldwide television audience of millions.

"Audrey? Do you know where you are?" Lydia asked.

"England! Mother England! Ain't she grand? God save the queen!"

This was not going to work. As Audrey danced off toward the wings and the backstage lights flashed, indicating thirty seconds until the show was back under way, Lydia looked around for someone to tell. Who? And what was she going to say?

Ah! There was Steven Goldhagen, headset on his head. She ran over to him. "Mr. Goldhagen?"

He frowned. "What? Make it quick!"

"There's a problem with Audrey Birnbaum. I don't think she can perform. In fact, I know she can't."

Steven looked as if he was going to be sick, but it took him less than two seconds to focus. "Tell me everything and tell me now." Then he spoke into his headset microphone. "Everyone? Get ready! Platinum may have to go solo. I repeat. Platinum may have to go solo."

Two minutes later, Platinum went solo, and two burly paramedics arrived. Lydia explained about the powder as best she could. "It will wear off," she promised them.

"We'll hook her up to an IV and watch her," one of the paramedics said. "Man, my kid would kill if I could get her autograph." They carried Audrey out on a gurney, on which Audrey was still boogying to her own beat.

Platinum went on by herself, seemingly unfazed that the duet she and Audrey had practiced for so long had turned into a solo. Lydia stood with her friends and watched, dumbfounded, as Platinum brought down the house with a performance that was absolutely fantastic. From there, the show got better and better. And by the time George Thorogood took the stage for the finale, an astonishing performance of "Bad to the Bone," where he was joined by just about everyone in the place who could sing, play, or dance, the latest edition of the Rock Music Awards achieved mythic status. Lydia, Kiley, and Esme were right there in the middle of the stage behind Thorogood, dancing their hearts out.

"You sure Audrey will be all right?" Kiley asked Lydia.

"Oh sure, I think everyone overreacted," Lydia said. "Not

that I'm happy that girl stole my stuff, mind you. What about you, Kiley? Sounds to me like you broke up with Tom for no good reason."

"And I don't think I can ever get him back," Kiley said sadly. "I wrecked it."

Esme pointed a finger at her. "Tonight is not the time to cry into your champagne."

"I agree," Lydia said, and linked arms with Kiley. "We are going to the mother of all after-parties. And we are going to find you the hottest guy there to make you forget that Tom Chappelle ever existed."

22

The Rock Music Awards after-party was right in the Hollywood & Highland complex, two floors above the Kodak Theatre at a nightclub called Level 3.

Thirty minutes after the show had ended, Esme found herself stuck in a mad crush near the Level 3 door. Security was so tight that the guards were scrutinizing everyone's invitations. Esme had heard that some nut had forged credentials for the Grammys after-party and, having gained access, fallen to his feet in front of Madonna and insisted that she make him her slave. If not her, then Alex Rodriguez. He was open-minded.

She was craning around, trying to spot Jorge in the crowd—she'd invited him to the awards, but he could only make the after-party—when she felt a warm hand on her back. There he was. He wore a black Ted Lapidus tuxedo, and looked so good he took her breath away.

"Where did you get a tux?" she blurted out.

He raised an eyebrow but looked amused. "That's how you greet me?"

"I didn't mean anything by it."

"Because I was hoping for something more like: 'Wow, you look great.' "

"You so do," Esme admitted. "I just . . . It's weird. Like it's you, but not you."

He considered that a moment as they edged toward the last security checkpoint. In front of them was George Thorogood himself, chatting with some rock chick. But Jorge seemed not to be dazzled in the least. "Well, that makes sense. Since we're us but not us like we used to be."

Heat rushed to Esme's face. "One date doesn't change anything."

He smiled. *"Mentirosa.* If you're not careful, I'll send you to Puerto Vallarta."

He had called her a liar, and he was right. She just didn't want to admit it.

When they finally made it through security, they entered a cavernous room with a large stage where Carlos Santana was leading his band in some sizzling music.

The two of them walked around, marveling at what they saw. There was a massive ice sculpture along one wall, with "Rock Music Awards" spelled out in glistening ice. Lemon martinis ran over the ice and into frosted martini glasses. Esme had never seen anything like it in her life. There was a huge sushi station where six uniformed chefs were making sushi and sashimi to order. Outside, on a balcony overlooking

Hollywood, was a massive Spanish tapas and dessert buffet, with more bartenders doing their thing.

"The rich are different from you and me," Jorge quipped as they headed back inside. Onstage, the band had just launched into the monster hit "Smooth" with Rob Thomas singing lead. People were already dancing.

"I love this song," Esme told Jorge over the music as she moved to the beat.

Before she could say more, a voluptuous woman in her forties threw her arms around Esme as if they were long-lost sisters, squealing her name. "Esme! How fabulous to see you!"

It was Beverly Baylor. Beverly was a major movie star who had been in the movie *Montgomery* with Jonathan. She'd hired Esme to do a freehand tattoo of a cowboy on her inner thigh. It was one of the tattoos that had truly gotten Esme's business off the ground. Beverly knew everyone and spoke to everyone.

Esme quickly introduced Jorge to Beverly, who then hiked up her lavender gown to display the tattoo.

"I get so many compliments," Beverly gushed. "I wish I could walk around naked so that the whole world could see it."

"Well, I'm sure the men out there would enjoy that," Esme said politely. Flattering her famous clients was something at which she'd become extremely adept.

"So, I haven't seen Jonathan lately," Beverly said. "What are you guys up to?"

Esme's eyes flicked to Jorge, who was unreadable, then back to Beverly. "Actually, Jonathan and I broke up."

"He dropped you," Beverly surmised. "That sucks."

That assumption *really* rubbed Esme the wrong way. Of course Beverly would think that the rich, gorgeous, semi-famous Jonathan would be the one to drop the poor brown girl. "Not really. I told him it was over."

She deliberately took Jorge's hand, and Beverly made some excuse about why she had to take off. Moments later, she had worked her way into the crowd.

"*Adiós!*" Jorge called.

"I stop being with Steven Goldhagen's son and I'm not worth much to her," Esme said.

"Do you care?" Jorge asked.

"Please. You know me better than that." She snorted.

"Yes, I do."

Esme realized this was true. Jorge knew her, the real her, not someone she was trying to be to please someone else. He wanted the best for her because he really knew her, got where she came from, and where she might be going.

"I want to show you something. Outside. It's too loud in here."

He nodded and led her through the crowd, which was growing larger by the minute, and outside into the humid night air. They dodged around Gwen Stefani, deep in conversation with Christina Aguilera about their respective children.

Once they were outside, Esme opened the clasp on her black satin borrowed-from-Warner-Brothers evening bag, took out a folded sheet of paper, and handed it to him.

"What's this?" he asked.

"You're in college. Read it."

"American Literature, Art History, Still Life and Life Drawing, Advanced Calculus," he read aloud. "Sounds like school."

"It's my class schedule," Esme explained. "For the High School of Visual Arts. They let you do a lot of the work over the Internet, so I won't have to spend much time at a building. The art classes meet at night. When I finish I'll have all the credits I need to graduate from high school."

"Impressive." To his credit, Jorge wasn't making that much of it.

"We'll see when I'm done. My parents will be happy, anyway."

"When will you tell them?" Jorge asked.

"Next week," she said. "I'm flying down for a visit."

He gave her back the schedule. "What about after school?"

"One year at a time. Please."

"Fair enough. But what made you change your mind?"

Now. Now was the moment to tell him.

"Back when I was in middle school and we lived in Fresno," she began softly, "I had my first boyfriend. Nick. He was older, in the Diegos. They were in a big war with the Razor Boys. My cousin Ricardo was a Razor Boy."

"I know those gangs," Jorge said.

"Nick taught me to drive. One day when I was driving with him next to me and two of his boys in the backseat, they shot my cousin Ricardo and three other Razor Boys coming out of a Taco Bell. They all died."

The image came back to Esme as if it had happened yesterday. She had spent so many years trying not to remember. Jorge was the first person she had ever told.

Esme went on, determined to spill the whole thing. "It was a setup. Nick wanted me to be driving when he murdered my cousin. Afterward he laughed and said it was payback. And he called me a whore." She swallowed hard. "For a long time, deep down I didn't think I deserved better because of what I had done."

"You were just a kid," Jorge pointed out gently, keeping his voice down. Esme realized that what they were talking about verged on the criminal. "And you didn't know what he was going to do."

Esme nodded. "So finally I figured, if I let that ruin my life, then it will be kind of like he killed me, too. And then, he wins."

Jorge pulled her to him. He didn't say a word, just held her close. And Esme felt, after all these years, that she was finally putting down a huge burden. She felt light, as if she could fly.

She felt free.

"What are y'all doing out here?" Lydia asked Esme and Jorge. They were standing outside in each other's arms, like some kind of statue. Esme seemed so relaxed. Jorge was hot in a tux. It was so sweet.

"Come on in and party!" Lydia insisted. She refused to take no for an answer. It wasn't every day that she and her friends appeared on national TV escorting famous rock stars off a stage. If that wasn't worth celebrating, nothing was.

When they got inside, Jorge said he'd get a plate of sushi for Esme and moved into the crowd. Lydia watched Esme watching him go.

"Shoot! Are you two together now?" she asked her friend eagerly.

"You have a way with words," Esme commented.

"Oh come on, sweet pea," Lydia said. "Tell me. Like, if you were comparing Jorge to Jonathan—"

"Stop!"

Lydia sighed. Esme really could be maddening. "What is the big, bad deal? Sex is one of my favorite topics."

"I am not sleeping with Jorge," Esme said, unable to keep the smile off her face. "As far as talking about sex goes, I'm sure you'll get plenty of practice when you're on tour with Audrey."

"Yeah, about that. You know how Audrey missed her duet with Platinum?"

"Yeah, what was that about?"

"Well, it seems she raided my guesthouse when she was staying at Kat's. I found out the hard way. Tonight."

"What did she take?" Esme asked.

"Hallucinogen. After about a couple of hours, it kind of paralyzes you for a while. Dang it. I told her my powders weren't recreational drugs, but she was just determined to see for herself."

"She'll be all right?" Esme asked.

"Oh sure, after a while it'll wear off. But for her to steal it? That's just *wrong*."

Esme nodded. "I agree with you."

"It kind of makes me think she isn't a real friend," Lydia concluded. "I mean, I got real dazzled by her, if you want to know the truth. That got me thinking about going on tour with her. I'd have to go where she wanted to go and do what she wanted to do, and I'm much too ornery to be under someone's thumb like that. Plus, I really did feel a little guilty about leaving my aunt in the lurch without a nanny. And there's school. Not that I go all that often, but it's the principle of the thing."

"You're staying?" Esme asked.

Lydia smiled. "At least here I'm my own woman. Plus, you know that lead guitarist of Dangerous Minds?"

"You escorted the band off the stage after they won Best New Artist."

"His name is Charlie. We got to talking, which led to flirtin', and he's taking me to a party in the Hollywood Hills tomorrow night."

Esme cocked her head at Lydia. "What about Flipper?"

"Oh, he's a big ol' sweetheart. So was Billy. I just don't think I'm a girl who's meant to be tied down."

"Ever?"

Lydia thought about that. "Ask me ten years from now," she decided as Jorge came back with a plate of sushi for Esme. Lydia plucked a slice of tuna off the plate, and looked around as she popped it into her mouth.

She was actually living the life she'd once only imagined from a mud hut. How great was that?

Kiley sat at the mirrored vanity in the ladies' lounge at Level 3. She'd already been there a long time. She adored the dress she was wearing—her very first floor-length gown. On one hand, she felt kind of like Cinderella at the ball. Just like Cinderella, having that amazing gown was temporary because she had to return it tomorrow. On the other hand, she felt more like one of Cinderella's stepsisters, because she'd lost out on the prince.

Kiley thought about how badly she'd treated Tom. How she was so insecure that she'd jumped to the conclusion that Tom was cheating on her in Russia with Marym. She did *not* want to be that girl. She thought about how nice he'd been to her from the very first day they met. She thought about how normal he was under all the glamor, how he'd waited until she was ready to have sex for the first time and hadn't pushed her. How he had been the one to help her get over the underwater panic attacks that for a few days had made it seem as though her dreams of a career as a marine biologist were just that: dreams.

Tom had trusted her, Kiley realized. But she hadn't trusted him. She had simply assumed the worst. She was ashamed of herself.

She stood. She couldn't mope in the ladies' lounge all night, even if that was what she felt like doing. She washed her hands in one of the black onyx sinks, then dried them on a rose-scented hand towel.

Tomorrow, she thought as she pushed through the ladies' lounge's massive cranberry leather double doors, *tomorrow I'll call him and see if I can get him to forgive me and—*

"Hey."

It was him. Standing right in front of her. Unlike most of the crowd, he wasn't dressed up. He wore faded jeans, a gray T-shirt, and sneakers.

"Lydia told me she saw you go into the ladies' room and that was . . ." He looked at his watch, then at her. "Twenty-three minutes ago," he observed. "I was about ready to come in after you."

"What are you doing here?" she asked, feeling off-kilter.

"I had an invite."

Right. Of course he had an invite. He was hot, young, and famous. This party was for the hot, young, and famous.

"I wasn't going to come. But then my bud Slade called me, so I went home, got my invite, and . . . here I am."

Slade wasn't exactly a common name. The only Slade Kiley'd ever met before was Slade Wayne, the model who was getting married.

"He told me everything, Kiley."

"Everything?" she echoed.

"You hanging out with Matt, and Matt convincing you that I was cheating on you."

Kiley could feel herself blushing. God, she felt so *stupid* all over again.

She cleared her throat. "I owe you an apology. I should have talked to you, instead of assuming—"

"Do you have any idea what I was going through? I couldn't figure out what the hell had happened while I was in Russia. I figured you'd met another guy, and that was why you were so cold. So I told myself, okay then, I'll move on, too. And I did."

A fist of misery shackled her heart. She deserved nothing better. What did she think, that she could treat Tom like shit and he'd live like a monk unless or until she decided to crook her little finger to beckon him? She'd never had that kind of self-confidence, and she probably never would. So, that was it, then. He'd stopped by to tell her in person that he was seeing someone else, that they were over. She was going to be strong and mature about this if it killed her.

"I hope the two of you will be very happy," she made herself say. "I should go find my friends now."

His words stopped her. "I went on one date with a makeup artist named Monica who reads tarot cards and lives on carrot juice. We went to Hermosa Beach but she wouldn't go into the water because it would mess up her skin. And all the time we were there, all I could think was: I wish she was Kiley."

"Because I don't usually wear makeup?" Kiley asked, her voice small.

"Because you're you. My dad? He's up at five every morning to feed chickens and milk cows. He and my mother have been married for twenty-five years. He doesn't bring her flowers or tell her how he feels about her, because he just figures she knows. I know that hurts her, makes her feel lonely—I can *see* that. I always said I'd be like my dad in the good ways, but not in the bad ways, and here I am—" He stopped midsentence. "Here I am making the same stupid mistake. Thinking you know. But how could you know when I haven't told you?"

Kiley could barely get the words out. "Told me what?"

"That I love you," Tom said. "I love Kiley McCann from La Crosse, Wisconsin. I love how genuine you are, and the freckles on your nose, and the way you laugh like a little girl. I love how much you love the ocean. I love how you smell. I love how you think. I love your face and every inch of your body and—"

"Stop," Kiley managed, but it was hard, because there were tears streaming down her face.

Tom looked bewildered. "You don't want to hear it?"

"Oh, I do," she assured him, laughing through her tears.

"But we're standing outside a bathroom. It's not exactly romantic."

He put his hands to her cheeks and gently wiped away her tears.

"I love you, too," Kiley said.

"Yeah?" he asked.

"Yeah. I've never said that before," she told him. "That's because I never felt it before."

He took her into his arms and kissed her until she was breathless. "I never said it before, either," he admitted.

Then the guy who made millions of women swoon kissed her again. But it didn't matter to Kiley anymore if they lusted after his billboards or called him or flirted with him on a movie set. Because he didn't love any of them. He loved her.

They went back into the party, which was now going at full decibels. It took them nearly fifteen minutes to find Lydia, Esme, and Jorge. They were out on the balcony with Steven Goldhagen.

Kiley saw how surprised her friends were to see Tom. Well, there was time enough later to explain it all to them.

"Kiley!" Steven exclaimed, motioning her over. "I was just asking about you."

Kiley quickly introduced him to Tom; Steven knew who Tom was and assured him he had a big future. Kiley was sure Esme had introduced Steven to Jorge as well.

"So, girls," Steven said, his gaze going from Esme to Kiley and Lydia. "I wanted to tell you what a terrific job you did this past week."

Lydia, as usual, had a ready reply. "Aren't you the sweetest? And by the way, we're also available for the Oscars."

Kiley was amazed at Lydia's audacity, but then, her audacity was one of the things that made her who she was.

Fortunately, Steven laughed. "If I produce the show I might take you up on that. Anyway . . ." He pulled a key from his pocket.

"What is the key for?" Esme asked.

"You know the swag room you set up? All kinds of gear is left over. Jewelry, jeans, shoes." He shrugged. "Stars. They have everything already."

"You want us to clean up?" Kiley tried not to look as disappointed as she felt. Oh well. They'd had a lot of fun.

Steven shook his head. "More like I want to show my appreciation for a job well done. Take the keys. Get some shopping bags. Go to town."

Kiley was sure she had misunderstood. "You mean we can pick something out? That's very nice of you."

Steven laughed. "Girls, it's all yours. Anything and everything."

Lydia turned to Tom and Jorge. "Gentlemen, if you would kindly talk among yourselves and excuse us ladies for just a tick, we need to take a little peek and then we'll come right back."

"I'll have my driver load the Mercedes and deliver the gear to your houses," Steven promised. "No worries."

Kiley wasn't sure her feet even touched the ground as she, Esme, and Lydia flew to the swag room. Esme unlocked the door; the girls walked in. And there it all was. Thousands and thousands of dollars' worth of stuff, stuff Kiley would never in a million years be able to afford. The shoes and the designer jeans and the high-end cosmetics and the jewelry. The free spa treatments and the iPhones and the CD players.

"Y'all, I think I just died and went to heaven," Lydia breathed. "This is the best day of my entire life."

"Me too," Esme agreed.

It was incredible. Kiley realized she was happy. And the wonderful, amazing thing was, she'd earned that happiness. She'd been brave enough to leave behind her small town, brave enough to come to Los Angeles and live here on her own. She was working hard to overcome her fears and her doubts and her insecurities. She'd risked loving a boy who most girls could only dream about.

Kiley knew there would be all kinds of problems, bumps, and bruises along the way. She still had her insecurities and she still hated her thighs and it would be an uphill battle to get into Scripps. But this she knew above all: she'd made friends with two of the most amazing girls to help her get through it.

"It's the best day of my life too," Kiley told her friends.

Before they went for the swag, they hugged each other. Because some things, Kiley realized, like the friendship they shared, glittered more than gold.

About the Author

Raised in Bel Air, Melody Mayer is the oldest daughter of a fourth-generation Hollywood family and has outlasted countless nannies.